I0451013

JUDITH

QUEEN'S BIRDS OF PREY BOOK 3

KATHI S. BARTON

This is a work of fiction. Names, characters, places, and incidents are products of the author's imagination or are used fictitiously and are not to be construed as real. Any resemblance to actual events, locations, organizations, or persons, living or dead, is entirely coincidental.

World Castle Publishing, LLC
Pensacola, Florida
Copyright © Kathi S. Barton 2020
Paperback ISBN: 9781951642822
eBook ISBN: 9781951642839
First Edition World Castle Publishing, LLC, June 22, 2020
http://www.worldcastlepublishing.com
Licensing Notes
All rights reserved. No part of this book may be used or reproduced in any manner whatsoever without written permission, except in the case of brief quotations embodied in articles and reviews.
Cover: Karen Fuller
Editor: Maxine Bringenberg

Prologue

The castle was going down, thanks wholly to her birds. Queen Dante sat upon her horse and watched as stone after stone crumbled to the ground. In a matter of moments, not only were the walls to the fort destroyed, but the king inside his castle was dead as well. Turning her mount, she headed back to the encampment to ready herself for the long ride home. The birds joined her not half an hour later, their large bodies covered in dust and blood.

"You have done well, my darlings." They could understand her and she them, but no one else could. She had made them what they were, and she would be the only one to control them. "Have you fed well on his dying cattle? How does it serve a man to have his food dying? His people, they were fed no better, I saw."

The falcon — she had never named them — told her that the people were headed west. In a few months or less, they would all be dead too. It bothered them when the people suffered because of the king or queen of the castle. But it was to be. Dante could not care for any more in her own keep.

No one would attack her keep. If they tried, she knew them to be too stupid or too drunk on their own mead. She had her birds, all of them bigger than life, made large by the magic that she had given them. Looking at them as they landed around her, forever keeping her safe, she wondered why she had not thought of it sooner when her king was still alive.

"I would have set you upon him. You could have eaten him for your dinner. Though I suspect it would have given you a great deal of belly pains." The hawk told her she was lucky he had died the way he had. No one would come for her if she had killed him. "Yes, that is absolutely true. But I suffered greatly when he was living. No children to give me comfort in my old age. I thought they might have been just like him, and that would have been too much to bear."

She would never marry again. Love wasn't anything she searched for. Not that she didn't have someone to warm her bed on occasion, but it was nice to be able to send them on their way when she had finished with them. Her heart belonged to no one, and she would not let another man take her to bed by force. All would be well. No one would threaten to come and take over her home, her birds' home as well.

The hawk used her beak to put delicate things upon the backs of the others. There was aplenty this time. Barrels and smoked meats. Pottery that they would use like it wasn't worth a king's gold. They raided the castle each time they conquered. Hawk was the best at getting in and out before they took the place to the grounds.

The eagle took off toward home. She would let the people know that Dante was returning simply by showing up. They would have a feast this night. The food upon her back would feed them for many days. The barrels of spices that had been hoarded in the lower levels of the castle would go a long way toward helping them trade what they did not grow.

The phoenix, by far the most deadly of her birds, shed her feathers in anticipation of getting new ones. After a battle, she would become anew, each time getting stronger, and her feathers, brilliant now, would be brighter still. She could flame a fire so hot that stone would crumble under a man's feet. The ground would no longer hold a seed within its belly to produce food, and she could kill a man with a single breath so that there would be nothing left of his body.

Dante loaded the last of her things onto the back of the owl. She might be small, she had always thought, but she could carry more than her own weight. And she would pick up her horse, used to flying through the sky like a bird himself, and take him back to the castle. He would be fed and groomed before Dante ever landed on the ground.

The vulture squawked at her, and she turned to look at the two men there. They looked as if they might have been about to kill her, but the sight of such large birds threw them off their duty. In no time at all, the vulture snapped both of them up and ate them down. A gruesome sight, but one that filled her heart with joy. She was safe again. The vulture took off too once she was loaded up.

"Well, my falcon, it is just you and I left." She told her that she was still armed. "Yes, well, probably not too bad of an idea seeing that they nearly shot us."

The falcon laid her body on the ground. She was the only one that was fitted with a seat, one that Dante rode on. Scouring the area, Dante made sure, as usual, that the place where she'd camped was as neat and clean as she'd found it—sometimes in better shape. As she climbed on the back of her bird, she held her breath.

"I do hate the height. I should have thought this through when I turned you into my warriors." Her laughter, should there have been someone around to hear it, might have caused someone to think her insane. "Homeward, my love, and we shall eat well tonight."

She took no one with her on her fights except the birds. That was why, she believed, her people were so loyal to her. She protected them, fed them better than herself, and made sure there was plenty for them to trade and share for things that she did not provide for them.

The soil was rich and would give forth a bounty like no other gardens. Flowers, too, that were woven into pretty things and traded. There was a smithy, as well as a doctor who doubled as a dentist. They had even acquired a gravedigger, who also doubled as a man who made markers.

There was a single merchant that came by. His wagon,

filled when he arrived, would be near empty when he left. He would bring the latest news with him, and any posts that he had been asked to bring. He would also, for a small coin, take out posts for the next time he was in the keep of a relative or friend.

And today, there was such a missive. But it was for her, from someone that she'd hoped never to hear from again—the king of all the land, the only man she answered to, though it wasn't with any kind of happiness on her part.

After the others were settled down, the food that had been brought put into storage, she sat down and wasn't surprised that the falcon came to see her. The room that she was in, the throne room for lack of a better term, had no roof and six perches for the birds when they wished to see her. Otherwise, they sat upon the top of the castle turrets, watching for anything that might befall them.

"I am to wed. The king of the land, he has decided that my castle is the best there is, and he will marry me himself." She asked about his castle. "He says that it will be his son's, which he has none of as yet. His last five wives only gave him daughters, from what I have heard, and they did not last long afterwards."

The falcon asked her what she would do. Dante knew what would happen to her should he come here. He would kill her. Being in her fortieth summer, she was much too old to bear any children now, and he would be better with a younger bride. One that could birth him the sons he wanted.

"He will kill me; we both know that. And you six will

kill him or be killed. I worry so much for the people here too." She thought of several plans and threw them out. It was in her head that if she were to die, she would do so on her own terms. "I will need a day to think on this. In the meantime, he says that he will be here in the new year. That will give us a month to provide for the people and make sure they are not harmed."

~*~

Dante worked as hard as the rest of her people. With her hair up in a rag, she didn't look any different than any of the men and women that toiled with her. There was much to be done in the little time they'd been allotted. Today they were drying all the beef and goat meat they had. It would last them for several months, and where she was sending them for safety, they'd need that extra time. Long enough for them to breed more of their cattle and goats so there would always be food for them to eat.

"What of the dried herbs that are left, my lady? There are already barrels of it packed away for the trip. Shall we put them in bags to go?" She shook her head. "There are no more barrels until the morn. What shall we do?"

"Leave them. There is extraordinarily little, correct?" The man said that there wasn't enough for a good strong stew. "Good. They will think you all died off from lack of planning, and that will keep you safe for a longer time. Leave it for them so that when the keep and castle are in ruin, the king will understand why."

Not that anyone was going to be coming to the castle to live, she thought. Things were in motion that would ensure everything here was gone well before the lands were walked upon again.

She looked to the sky when a dark shadow fell over her. Her hawk was making her way to the village Dante had set up. Long ago, Dante had purchased the lands far from where she was now and put them in the name of Mercy Dante. She knew so much about all their futures that it made her so sad to know she'd never be there to see it happen.

"My lady?" She looked at her man of arms, a man who had extraordinarily little work to do but was brave and true to her. "We have plenty of things to go on the next load if you have a desire to send it on. Do you still wish for some of the armed men to go with them this time? I'm to understand that we're to fell trees for homes."

"Yes, that would be good. How many men can you spare today?" He told her all that she had. "Then send them on. I know some of you are frightened to ride the birds, but you should have no fear. They would no more harm you than they would me." He nodded and looked at her hawk. "I shall send you all on her. She is the most gentle of the six of them."

The carrier had been fashioned a week ago. It had upset her that it had taken so long to get right, but it was safe now, and that was all she wanted. There were only a few short weeks to get the people gone from here with all that would keep them safe. Now all she had to do was make sure the birds didn't know the last of her plans.

The platform had been made from several drawbridges

from castles that they'd taken over. She'd known that saving them would be helpful, but it had taken a great deal more work than she'd thought it would to put them together and have her fishermen weave a netting to carry it with. After several trials and failures, the carrier worked.

Loading up the men on the first run of people, she noticed they had put the several men that were afraid of the ride in the middle. One of them, a hardy man otherwise, had been knocked out with much wine. It had been funny to all around that it had taken so little of the wine to do that to him. But they didn't know that she'd given him a bit of magic to help him travel. All was well when her hawk took off with the several dozen men to start on the homes that would be needed.

Barrels would be next. They had been sealed by magic that would keep them well preserved. The other birds, her warriors for all time, had been taking jewels and other items to a cave she had also covered in magic. It would help the people of the new village for as long as they lived. Well beyond her body being nothing but dust.

Dante watched as several more people were taken to the new village. She would allow them to name their new place as long as it would never be attached to the name of the castle. That would be bad for them and would bring much trouble onto their heads. When her hawk landed, she went to ask how things were progressing.

"Well, my lady. They were off the platform for mere seconds when they started to work. I believe you were good to get them started on this. 'Tis only late autumn, so they should be able to have a few of the buildings up before the rest are moved." Dante agreed with her. No one else could understand the birds but her and the other birds. It had, she knew, kept everyone safe all these years. "I can only make two trips there and back, my lady. 'Tis not a long way by the way we fly, but the pack is heavy. Please forgive me for that."

"You have nothing to be sorry for, my bird of prey. You have done one more than I had hoped for this day. And when the others have finished their tasks for me in carrying away the riches and other things the people will need, it will take no time at all to move the rest. Nay, you have done well this day in taking the men, and then the food to feed them while there." Her hawk, who would someday be called Blaze, bowed before her.

Stacking up the loads that would be going on the platforms, she could see that they'd be taking away the last of it only the day before the king was to arrive. Dante was glad now that she'd had such good people working for her. They asked nothing as to why they were doing this but did it for her. When in reality, it was all for them and her birds.

Dante knew the king would never make it here. His ship and all his bounty would be deep in the waters he crossed to kill her and take her castle. The man was a fool to think she would easily do what he wanted. Wiping at a tear, she looked around the keep she'd worked so hard to keep everyone safe in. It was then that she saw her son.

Duncan was everything she was and more. Each time she saw him, she would give him a little more of herself, teach him something of running a castle. He knew what he was to her, and that Mary was doing her a great favor in keeping him safe. Duncan would be a greater king than she ever was a queen, just the way it should be. She was glad now that she'd told him he was to be mated to one of her birds.

Leaving him to his work, she entered the castle to see what else was there that she could easily live without. There was truly little left as it was, but she moved from room to room to make sure nothing was left behind of any value. The only thing she could see in the great room was the painting of herself.

Dante wished so many times that she could have put her son there with her, but it was not to be. It would have been foolhardy to think she'd be able to keep him safe if she was to put out there that he'd been born. Other kingdoms would have done a great many things to have captured him to bring her to heel. Dante would do anything to keep him safe, including submitting to a man again. A thing she would never do again in her lifetime.

"I shall give this to our falcon." She turned her head enough to find Duncan behind her, and the doors closed to anyone walking around. "She will be a great person, I think. Sour to many except the one she will love."

"You have seen this?" Duncan said he'd seen a great many things. "Well, you know as well as I that it might not turn out the way we see it. There can be changes, you know."

"This I am aware of. As well as you not living past the

last person that is taken from here." She turned to look at him then, trying to see just what he was seeing. "I shall forever miss you, Mother."

It was the first time he'd called her that. Her heart, so tender of late, made her burst into tears at all that would be gone in so short a time. Hugging him to her, she knew the strength in his body was getting stronger daily. He knew how to work and did it without complaint.

"I have been writing a book. It is just for you, my son. You will know things I have known for some time. It will replenish the riches that I have put aside for you. Also explain how to keep the birds safe should they need it." He nodded. "I will give it to Mary on the day you travel. I do not want the others to know you are my son, even after all is finished here."

"They will only know me as a man you trusted. But I will need to tell them at some point. This, you know as well as I. I will be their king when they need me." She nodded, tears flowing quickly now. "Mother, you do know that I will take care that they are as safe as you made them here?"

"I do, my son. I know that better than you could. You are not anything like your father, a cruel and terrible man. When you marry, and you will, I want you to know that she will only love you if you give her your heart. It's important that you do that for her." He said he would. "Let her strength help you when you know that you are not armed to do it on your own. She will love you more and respect you forever for that."

"Will she be stronger than me, Mother?" Dante told

him she was sure of it. "Then I will be for her what you have been for these people—a person of worth. I promise you I will also protect her forever."

"That is all that anyone can do for their mate, my child." He hugged her, something that neither of them were able to do often. "I shall miss you, Duncan. Much more than I could ever explain to you. Go forth, protect all the people of your kingdom, and do what I say. Love your mate more than anyone, including yourself, and the two of you will be able to move mountains."

~*~

New Town, what they had begun to call the new place they were living, looked like any other town in the country. The only difference was, this one was only several weeks old. It, to Dante, looked as if it had been established long ago. She was pleased with the work her people had given the place she'd moved them to.

"My lady? There is a problem in one of the homes we've put up. I know how to fix it, but the man living in it, he said that he will be fine with it. To have his own home was more than he could have hoped for." The queen of the people asked Barron what the issue was. "He has five daughters, my lady, and we've somehow put him into a house with only one bedroom. There are ones he could use, but he insists that they be used for the other families."

"I shall speak to him. Is it Donald, the mule man?" Barron nodded, his face nearly touching the ground, he was bent so much. "Stand up, man. I believe I have pointed out that this is not a time for formality. We must all work together for the greater good of the people. I shall speak to him now. Then I must, as you know, return to the castle for the final loading."

Along the way to speak to Donald, she was stopped no less than twenty times to be thanked for the things she'd provided for the people. Without making the great move, Dante knew all of them would have been killed. Because of their loyalty to her as queen of the castle, the king of these realms, a tyrant of a man, would have ordered them all butchered as soon as he killed her on their wedding night. Of this, she was certain.

"My lady? I have yet to put on a pot for tea, but you must join us in it." Dante was not one to hold back when she had something to say. She told Donald she wanted him to take a larger home. "Oh, my lady. Barron should never have bothered you with this. We are quite happy with where we are."

"But you have six people in a single man's home, Donald. What, I ask you, will the man who was supposed to be in this home do with a home with many bedrooms? He will be overwhelmed in trying to keep them clean while you are smashed up in this one bedroom chamber with your little girls." Donald looked at his daughters, beautiful little ones that were his pride and joy. "There is a home just over the road here you shall be moved to. I insist. Your daughters will share two bedrooms, and you will have your own. I know for a fact, sir, that your snore is legendary. For your daughters to have a good sleep, you will need to be far from them. Do you not agree?"

"Yes, my lady." He moved just a little closer, and in a low voice spoke to her. "I did not wish to cause you any undue trouble. You have given all of us a chance to survive this, and I wanted to be sure you knew I was ever so grateful for it. I'm as happy here with you and yours as I ever was in the castle keep, my lady. Incredibly happy."

"I'm glad that you're happy here, Donald. You are a good man and a man that cares well for his daughters. I shall have the men move you to the new home. It will give me a good feeling knowing you have plenty of room for yourself and your family." He thanked her. "Your daughters, sir, they will be safe here. You need anything, you make sure that you contact Barron."

"Thank you, my lady. If there is ever anything I can do for you, you need only to ask. I am and will be indebted to you for the rest of my days." Dante felt her eyes water up with the man's words. Her life, she knew, was only a short time away from ending. "Thank you very much."

The little girls curtsied at her, and she had to move on. It broke her heart every time she saw small children. She so wanted to hold her own. Telling Donald she'd have the men move him once again, she moved toward the long house that would serve as a church for the people and a meeting place for them to gather should they need to. Her eagle was awaiting her when she returned to the now all but abandoned castle.

"You have done well, my heart. You, of all the birds I have, are the one I worry most about." The eagle asked her why. "You are so much like me. Hard when you're needed to be. Too soft when it comes to our people. I fear someday it will harm you in ways that not even I could fix."

Her eagle, like the other birds, had been a huge part of getting the people moved. If not for them, there would be no way she could have done this. It would have meant certain death for all of them, including her own son.

Going to the throne room, she sat upon the floor. Dante had moved her chair to the caves for the others to sell off should no one want it. But because she could see into the future, just bits and pieces, she knew that at least one of them would want such a monstrosity.

"When this is finished, soon now, I will give you and the other birds magic to keep you safe from others who would try and capture you." Her eagle asked what sort of magic. "You will be able to blend into situations you wouldn't normally consider a problem. There will be problems, too. From the things I have seen, you all will have trouble from those around you."

She laid back on the cold stone. The castle had been forged so long ago, Dante could not remember who had erected it. Now, as she looked up into the night sky, the roof here long since removed, she thought of what was going to happen in the coming days.

"He has set sail and is nearly here. The king of all the lands is coming to claim not just my castle and my wealth, but my birds as well. There are many people on the vessel that carts his bottom here who have no desire to be his servants. If only I could have saved them as well." The eagle, standing upon her perch built just for her, reminded her she could not save them all. "In this, I wish it was wrong to have thought that. They will suffer, these people. They are suffering, for there is nothing to do to appease the king to find favor with him. There are few that he has not made suffer by lashing them on their backsides. Too many of them have died in his foolishness to make me his wife for such a short time."

Listening to her eagle squawk at her about the king and idiocy, Dante thought of her impending death. It would be a sad affair only to her son and the birds he would one day claim as his own. However, just knowing all would be safe from the king's tyranny made all the other things so worthwhile.

"If I had it to do again, I would do nothing differently. I would still do what I am doing now so that all would live on. Even with you birds, I would do just what I have done to keep my kingdom here." The eagle asked her if she'd been happy. "Happy? I don't know that I have had that much happiness in my lifetime. I have been content. Not the same, I suppose, but I have been content with my lot in life. If only I could have kept living the way that we have, I do believe I could have made such a difference in things here and in the future. Before I forget this again, I have taken the time to write out the things t'will keep the new town with coin in their coffers. I know it will be aplenty, but I will worry until my last breath if it will be enough."

Her last breath. It was only a few days away. Much too soon for her, but also, Dante knew, it would be well worth the pain of dying. Sitting up, she looked at the birds, all six of them on their perches watching over her and the emptied lands that they could see. They were the sole reason she was able to do this. This she knew more than anyone could have guessed.

"I shall retire, I think. I have no bed to speak of now, so I will only lie upon the ticking. On the morrow, we shall have a feast. A great amount of food, as well as drink. 'Tis fitting, I think, to celebrate this new way of life for so many." Her beautiful phoenix asked her why she seemed so sad. "Sad? Aye, I am that and more. Things are moving at a pace I wish didn't exist. But it is for the wellbeing of all that have called this place home. In that, I suppose I am sad that I shall never be able to return here in my lifetime."

But they would. All six of them and more would return someday and see the castle as it should have been—a lovely home to her son and his mate. The one that she herself had hand-picked for her beloved child. Oh, to be able to see them grow into love. But it was not to be.

Getting up before she made a fool of herself by crying over something she had no control over, Dante did indeed head to her bed. For tomorrow and the next would be the hardest of anything she'd ever done before.

Chapter 1

There was no hope to salvage anything from the burnt out shell of a house. Someone had set it; Jude was well aware of the smell of gasoline within the place. It sickened her that someone had waited until everyone was busy getting ready for Christmas and the holidays to deliberately set fire to the house.

Jude looked up when her sister Piper said her name. "I'm going to burn this to the ground. Just so when the place is rebuilt, they don't have to worry about cleaning up the area. Have you found anything yet?" Jude told Piper she'd not found anything at all but a few broken items. "I can smell the gasoline that was used. I'm assuming you already knew."

"I did. Have you heard anything from the family? I've not." Piper told her just what she knew—the family was staying in the house down the road until they could rebuild. "Do you think they did this on their own? I have to admit, it was very telling when we found the kitchen devoid of anything other than a few cans of dog food. Smells fishy even to me."

"Why don't you just say it? It smells like they did this to reap from their insurance policy. The trouble with this is, they might just be able to get themselves a brand new home. Did Mercy tell you they've done this before? Maybe I should burn down my house and start over. There wouldn't be any lingering gas smells either." They both laughed. "But seriously, what do we know about this family? Other than they're arsonists."

"Just what Mercy told us. This is the second time they've had their house burn down around them. The last time they were only able to get partial help on the rebuild because a large portion of the house was salvageable. This time, in my opinion, they made sure there was nothing at all left to build from." Piper looked around when Jude did. "The Christmas thing is still a few days away. Are you leaving early with the rest of the family? I've not decided when I'm going. I don't even know where we're going to be staying when we get there."

"I'm not leaving early. I have one more piece to finish, then I'm going to ship it to the show I'm having in January. I know I could carry it. It's for a charity event I signed up for about six months ago. I'm not in the mood to even go, much less bring an item to auction for people to pay extraordinarily little for. That sounded like I was bitching because I didn't want to help. But it's just...I don't know. I'm not really in the mood for Christmas, I guess you could say. I'm hoping that once we get there, that'll put me in the spirit." Jude told Piper she had sounded ungrateful. "I'm not upset, actually. Ungrateful? I guess just a little. I'm not used to having to share my sisters. It's been just us six for thousands of years. About the party? I guess you could say I'm indifferent to going. I love the holidays when we six get together. This will be the first time in longer than anyone in our town can remember that we'll not just be the birds celebrating the holiday."

"We'd have Joel, Miley, and Bryson this year. I don't mind them being here. However, going someplace that is so strange to us doesn't make it feel like a fun holiday for me." She grinned at Piper. "I'm giving Miley the most outrageous gift. I hope she likes it. It's my old medieval armor that I wore a long time ago. She talks about the one you have in your home all the time."

"See? That, right there, is what I'm talking about. No one there will have any idea that it's something you wore, and are giving it to a kid you love like we all do." Piper picked up a large burnt piece of wood. "This reeks of gas. I think the fire marshal needs to come here and have another look around. I know he was here before, but I'm telling you right now, if his report says anything but arson, I'm going to boil him in his own fat."

They both turned when a car pulled into the driveway. The emblem on the side proclaimed him to be the same man the two of them had just been talking about — the fire marshall, Aryne Patterson. He nodded to Jude and stared at Piper. Everyone was blown away by their beauty when they saw them for the first time, but Jude thought the man was staring directly at Piper's hair. To her, it looked like Piper had dipped her head into the setting sun over an open body of water, the colors were so bright with the hues of the late sunlight.

Piper, like her, was a bird. Jude was an eagle. Piper was a phoenix. It was why her hair was so breathtaking. Her hair, like the others, was what her feathers looked like when she shifted to her other half. It was just as bright, if not brighter, when the phoenix came out to play. Clearing her throat before the man got himself in dutch with Piper for staring so long, Jude asked him why he was there.

"Lady Oliver asked me to come by, today if I could, to look the house over before it was taken the rest of the way down. I had no idea the family was in such a hurry to rebuild. I came as soon as I could." Jude thanked him. "No reason to thank me, Lady Jude. This is my job. I'm to understand that you and the other ladies are going out of town for the holidays. I so wish my family could do that once in a while. Go visit other relatives, I mean. I hate all the fuss and bother with having so many people in my home."

Piper laughed, and Jude did as well as the little man came to stand in what Jude thought was the living room. Not speaking to him while he worked, she moved to stand with Piper to speak to her.

"Mercy said you were going to sell your condo. Have you had any luck in finding a place you'd like to live?" Piper said that all the good homes were taken by Mercy and Blaze. "Yes, well, I'm sure they didn't take them all.

I'm looking as well, but I have to admit, I'm in no hurry to buy just yet. I love a couple of houses here, but they're very drab to me. I want something old like Mercy's home, and as homey as Blaze's. They both have the best taste in decorating a room. Don't you think?"

"Yes. I suppose. I think with Blaze, however, she has some extra help in the décor of the house. I'm thinking Bryson has a lot do to with the things in the living room. I've never been so tempted to take a nap as I am when I sit on their couch. It doesn't even matter if the fireplace is lit, I feel all warm and cozy when I'm there." Jude said she had the same feelings. "I'd steal them from her if I thought I could get away with it. I guess I'll have to go and buy me a set of them so I can have some too."

"How nice of you."

They were both laughing when the fire marshall asked them what they knew about the family. After Piper finished giving him what she knew, Jude told him the rest. "This is their second fire. This time I'm to understand they have an exceptionally large policy on their home and contents. Also, I don't know if this matters to you or not, but when the house was inspected two months ago when they doubled their insurance, the value of the home didn't meet the criteria for what they were insuring. I'm not sure what happened as to whether they were able to upgrade the policy or not."

"They were turned down. But I have since found out the family was able to get a second policy from someone out of state. Once this is settled, not in their favor, I'm thinking, the secondary insurance company will have to surrender their license to sell homeowners' insurance. This is not going to go well for the Martins, I'm afraid." He turned to look at the two of them. "Lady Piper, can you tell me your opinion of the fire? I know you to be an expert on fires. I would greatly appreciate your insight on this one."

"Do you smell the gasoline?" He nodded at Piper. "Then I believe you have your answer. I would also like to point out we've not found any furniture except a beaten up couch in the basement. There are no frames we can find for any mattresses, nor much in the way of food in the kitchen area to your right. Also, and I find this really weird, there isn't a single television shell or anything in the way of picture frames with broken glass. There should have been at least one that would have survived, I think."

"I noticed there isn't a washer and dryer here, either." Piper told him she'd not thought of that. "Yes, well, you haven't been doing this for as long as I have. I believe, however, eventually, you would have noticed it."

"Thank you." The man looked around at the large barn, as well as the three storage sheds in the back of the property. He asked if they'd been in them. "We haven't. I wasn't aware that we could."

"I can. It is my job to be as thorough as I can when inspecting a place after a fire. I would very much like it if you two were to go with me while I open them." He smiled at them. "I seemed to have lost the note that was given to me just this morning on those buildings in the back. I don't remember if it said I should or shouldn't look inside of them. The contents belonged to someone else in the family. The sir's mother, I think?"

"She's no longer alive." He nodded. "Oh, I see. You lost the note. I understand now. Yes, Piper and I will be only too happy to go out with you to the shed. But I'm thinking, just to be sure we don't cause any harm to the building's contents, we should call the police as witnesses to it."

"Great idea, Lady Castle. Yes, I think you might well be onto something with that."

Piper called the police, and the three of them waited for them to show up. Piper, like the rest of the birds, was on incredibly good terms with every cop on the force. When you donated enough money for them to have an entirely new building built, they didn't mind coming around for little things like this. The inspection of a couple of buildings and the probable outcome would tickle them.

The police showed up in less than five minutes. After Mr. Patterson told them what he was doing and what he needed to do, it was the police who broke the large lock on the barn door to open it. He, Officer Dent, told them his body camera was on, and he'd make sure the insurance company had a copy of it before he left today.

As soon as the lock was broken and the chains pulled away, Officer Dent opened the door and whistled. Jude didn't have to look to know that the barn was filled with the things from the house. She followed Piper into the building after the two men entered.

"It's marked with their rooms." That was what she noticed too. Piper walked to one of the boxes labeled kitchen and pulled out several cans of green beans. "This is why there aren't any cans of food in the house. They've saved all their things out here. I'm betting that someplace in here is all their photo albums, as well as some pieces of furniture."

"The furniture is over here." Piper just looked at her when Officer Dent claimed he'd found more things at the back of the barn. "I'm going to have our police photographer come here and take pictures of this stuff before we leave here. Also, I'm not sure what you think, Mr. Patterson, but I'm thinking this is fraud."

"It is. I guess I thought they might prove to just be unlucky people. However, it's very noticeable, they're crooks. My work here is finished. I'm going to mark it as arson and put the suspects in the family here where it asks me." He shook his head. "The things people think they can get away with makes me sad at times."

The photographer showed up about twenty minutes after Mr. Patterson left. The man said what he'd found here today was going to be taken up in court. Jude was only glad someone else had noticed what she'd thought all along. The people that lived here had taken a huge chance in setting this fire. Should one of the police or fire personnel have been hurt, it would have been prison time, she was positive of it.

After inviting Piper to dinner with her, the two of them decided to just eat some burgers instead of fighting the holiday crowd to get into a sit down type of restaurant. Even the place they picked was busier than she thought it would have been on a Thursday night.

It was getting cold now. A bit before Christmas, she had hoped it would be just a little warmer for the children who were going to be at the castle for the holiday. Jude asked Piper if she knew how much they'd donated to the party.

"No. I know Mercy said it was a great deal, but her great deal and mine are vastly different, I've come to figure out." Jude laughed. "Having one of you guys put the price on my work is the only reason I'm making any kind of money. I would tell someone where all the flaws were, as well as not charge them nearly enough as I could get for each of the pieces."

"I've noticed that about you. Two weeks ago, when you had me come out to the studio, you told me you were thinking of only five hundred bucks for the Indian at Rest piece. I had an idea that you hadn't put enough zeros on it. It sold immediately, if I remember. Piper, I find it hard to believe you undervalue your work so much." Piper told her she thought a lot of artists did the same thing. "I guess. As you said, you'd be pointing out all the flaws in something you've made. All I see when I look at your work—and I would imagine anyone looking at it would see the same— is perfection."

Their food was brought to them, and they both dug into their burgers and fries. When Jude thought of all the calories she was shoving in her face, all she could be thankful for in that moment was the fact that she'd not gain an ounce from it. Laughing to herself, she thought she might have a brownie sundae while she was at it.

"I was thinking about this party thing. Why do you suppose Mercy thought it was a good idea for us all to go?" Jude asked Piper what she meant as she pushed her empty plate away. "I don't know. Didn't she seem kind of pushy about us all going to this? I was going to go anyway— anything to help out kids during the holidays. However, I got the feeling if I said I wasn't going to go, she'd have a fit about it. It's probably just me. I've been feeling slightly overwhelmed by a lot of shit lately."

"No. I didn't notice. But then, I won't argue with her. If I didn't want to go, I'd simply not say anything to her and just stay home. I'd get bitched at later about it, but I'd get to stay home. Why are you overwhelmed? To be honest, Piper, so am I. I think it's about getting a house. We're the only two looking for one. Everyone else has this mansion of a place, while we're still in apartments." Piper told her that might well be it. "Are you still looking for a place closer to your studio?"

"No. I've decided when I do find myself a home, I'm going to build a studio there. I'm really getting sick of going all over the place to work, then eat or whatever I need to do on the way home or to the grocery." Jude laughed with her. "I'm telling you right now, if I ever find my mate, I'm not going to be all sappy around him. Mercy looks at Bryson the same way people look at cute puppies. It's gross."

They were still sitting there an hour later, just catching up on things. It wasn't as if all of them didn't see each other several times a day, but Jude was enjoying the one on one conversation between just the two of them. She thought she might like to do this more often. Find one of the others just to hang out.

~*~

Duncan walked around the house three times to make sure everything was where it was supposed to be. No food was on the tables yet, of course, but they were ready for it. The trees had been up for the last week and a half, and he couldn't help but marvel at how festive they made the rooms look. Picking one of the gifts off the tree, he smiled when he saw how it had been wrapped — or not wrapped, in this instance.

Someone in the house had taken the time to make each of the cash gifts, twenty-five dollars, into origami ornaments. It was both clever and cute at the same time. He would have to remember to thank everyone for the extra effort being put forward for this celebration.

"Your lordship, there is a phone call for you. It's the balloon company again." Duncan didn't laugh out loud, but he had to work hard at not doing it. "They have called here several times now. Do you think they do not understand English?"

"I'm sure they do. But last night, I decided to take them up on the offer of having twice the number of balloons on site. I'm sure he's just making sure." Nodding, Alexander walked away. Duncan made his way to the phone.

After dealing with the man about the balloons, Duncan walked around the rest of the rooms on the main floor. It was going to be quite fun, he thought. Pausing in front of the portrait of his mom, he told her how much he loved her and wished she was there too. It was the woman he was going to meet that had him so nervous, and he told her that.

Duncan spoke to his mom daily. Even with all the brouhaha going on, he still made time to sit and have a conversation with her. It was a comfort for him to talk to her, even though he thought the rest of the household thought him off his rocker. Today, this time, was no different. He smiled up at her when he took his usual seat to talk.

"Judith will be here in a couple of days. I'm as nervous as I've ever been in my life. To think, so long ago, you knew who was going to be my other half." Alexander, his butler, friend, and someone he depended on a great deal sat him down a cup of tea, as well as some scones fresh from the oven. Taking one, Duncan looked up at his mom. "I've been able to locate the ring. I don't know if you remember or not, but I had mislaid it. I didn't lose it so much as I didn't have it in the first place. I remembered, of course, after I found it. I had sent it to be cleaned several days beforehand. I'm so glad they sent it to me, or I don't know how much more I would have had to look through the things you left for me."

He thought about the gifts he'd gotten for the birds. "I've put them in the kind of wrapping paper I knew you'd get a kick out of. I've also made sure that Miley gets the other crown, as you asked me to do. Every day you have had me do one chore or another, and I feel so much closer to you than ever before."

When he'd located his mother's book, he'd not had

much time to look it over. When they'd first moved to New Town, Duncan read it from cover to cover. Sometimes he'd read some passages over and over. Not that he wanted to read any words she'd put to paper for him back then, but he'd been grief stricken by her death. However, now she had a daily chore for him to do with the Christmas party she'd told him to have. Today he was to rest. He was no better at that then she'd been, he thought with a grin.

"When she gets here—well, perhaps not exactly when she arrives—I'm going to ask her to marry me." He had rethought that several times over the last days. "Or I'll have her propose to me. I don't know yet. However, I do know that she is going to make the perfect queen for us. She's the most beautiful creature ever made. With the exception of you, Mom."

Duncan didn't think he was off his noodle in talking to his mom daily. He had a good head on his shoulders, and he'd been highly educated, having gone to several colleges in his lifetime. Duncan thought himself easy to get along with as well. But he was sure of one thing. Every thought, every word he'd been practicing to say to Judith, would go out the door when he laid eyes on her close up.

"I'm going to be worse than a small school boy, all tongue-tied and everything. I swear to you, Mom, I'm going to make a total fool of myself, you just watch and see." He laughed at himself. "I've seen other men with their loves. I would love to say that I'm not going to be so sappy around her, but I have a feeling it's a male thing, and I'll be so much more sappy than any other of my genre."

After telling her everything he'd done since their last talk, Duncan made his way outside. Out here was where most of the decorations were being put up. Standing back out of the way of the workers, Duncan thought it looked just like he'd envisioned it, like a castle made of fun and sweets.

The children, twelve of them in total, not counting the men and women that were there to help, would be arriving on the morning of Christmas. He had thought to have them spend the night in the castle, but it wasn't to be. The red tape he had to go through to simply have a party for them had nearly taken all his time. The gifts also had to be approved by the home the children were going back to.

"Your lordship?" He turned and looked at Billy. The young man, William Sheets, had been with him since he'd had the renovations started on the castle and the keep surrounding it. "I've been looking around, and I don't think there is a single thing out of place. Mayhap you need me to do something else?"

"No. You have the plans, correct?" He showed him that he had them. "Good. You just keep things like it says in the book there and we'll have the best decorated castle in the world. Don't you think?"

Billy grinned at him, then walked away. He had been born with a disability, but it hadn't stopped him from being a great person. Every time he saw Billy's mother, when she'd come to get her son or just to drop him off, Duncan would tell her what a wonderful job she'd done in raising him. He was not just a joy to be around, he took his work seriously.

Going back to his office, he started looking over some of the paperwork from the last few days. Duncan needed to get some work done, or he'd not have things finished up in the coming year. Excitement was making him lazy, he thought with a grin.

Not only did he run several businesses, but Duncan also had an exceptionally good portfolio. His mom, in seeing the future, had told him what to buy and how much it would be worth. Even without the stash his mom had left him, Duncan made enough money on other ventures that he was able to not touch the gems and gold and live on what he made now.

Deep in thought of what he was reading, when his phone rang, he picked it up without looking at the caller identification. As soon as he heard the heavy breathing on the other end, he closed his eyes and waited for the man to start spewing his rhetoric to him.

"If one of them damned kids comes anywhere near my property, I'm going to shoot first, then I'm going to sue you. I told you when you got that stupid idea in your head, I wasn't going to tolerate it." Duncan said nothing. "You hear me, young man? I'm not joking with you at all. I see one foot on my side—"

"I have six thousand acres here, Mr. Bloom. I'm willing to bet my life on the fact that not one person will step anywhere close to your place." Mr. Bloom had been a pain in his backside from the moment Duncan had started renovating the castle to its original form. Bloom told him he'd be keeping an eye on it. "You do that. In the meantime, Merry Christmas, you old goat." Duncan then hung up.

Normally he would never have spoken to a human like he had with Mr. Bloom. But there were times when Duncan despaired of ever having the man just relax on his side of the property line. He'd even invited the grouch over for the party, and he'd heard an earful about that too. Christ, there just wasn't any way to please the buzzard.

At almost midnight, Duncan got up to stretch. He didn't need to sleep, so he would roam the halls late at night and make plans. He had always thought he had the best ideas when he was the only one around. Stopping in front of the large painting of his parents, Duncan wondered what his mother had been thinking when she'd had to sit so close to his sire.

The painter had captured his mother's pain quite well. The hand on her shoulder, the one his sire had put on her, was clenched deeply into Mom's flesh. Duncan always wondered if Mom had been bruised by the grip at her shoulder. Knowing it would have been something she carried for at least a few hours made him hate his sire all the more. Duncan had heard all the stories about his sire and was glad he'd died before he was born.

The next row of paintings brought him to the grandparents. Lord and Lady Beswick had been his mother's parents. He knew a little about them, but not too much. Duncan also thought they were still alive someplace. If only, he thought, if only I could contact them and let them know I am alive and well.

Just as he was turning from the painting, something moved at the corner of his eye. Duncan turned in that direction slowly. Whatever it had been, or in this case whoever it had been, was still standing in the long hall in front of the very picture he had been looking at. When the specter smiled at him, his knees simply went out on him, and he fell to his ass.

"Mom?" She nodded at him, then pointed to her parents. "What are you...? How are you here?"

"I visit you on occasion. I thought today of all days I'd speak to you, son. I wish for you to find them—your grandparents on my side. They are alive and have been living poorly in a ramshackle place. You need to find them. Bring them here." He said he would. "I mean, for the wedding. I would like for you and Jude to find them and bring them here for the wedding. You know just where they are, Duncan. We visited them there when you and Mary and I went on a little adventure."

"The cottage?" She moved closer to him as she nodded. "Mom, if you've been here before, why haven't you ever let me see you? I would have given anything to have seen you. I've missed you every day I've been alone."

"You talk to me. That has been enough—for now, at least. Mercy will tell you great stories about me, but do not let her be sad. She's hard enough to live around, I would think, without her being all sad and despondent. She is and always will be the best person I know to help you with finding them." Duncan said he'd contact her today. "Good. Also, I want you to stop talking to me every day. You're beginning to repeat yourself, and I'd rather you weren't committed when you have my grandchildren about. You will have them, will you not?"

"I think we should leave that up to Judith. Don't you?" His mother laughed. It made him smile that he would know her laughter anywhere. Mother laughed like a braying jackass, as Mercy had said about her. "Mom, I miss you so much. I know the birds do as well. Can you come to see them while they're here?"

"I cannot, my heart. I cannot. It would be painful for me to see them and not be able to hug them as women. They saved my life and my kingdom more times than I think there are numbers. Oh, how I wish I could touch them once more. To take the memories of seeing them back with me."

Mom turned away from him before she asked him to come with her. He followed his mom's ghost to the bottom of the stairs. While standing in the living room, she moved to the fireplace. It was just on the tip of his tongue to tell her to be careful of the flames when she spoke to him again.

"See that stone there? I wish for you to push it hard when they arrive here. First thing, all right, my son? This is all for my birds, Duncan. I have come here today so that you could show them this chamber and allow them to take what I have collected for them." He asked her if he should go, as well. "Yes, that would be lovely. I want you to know I did not suffer much when the stones began to fall on me. Hardly at all, as a matter of fact. Because I wanted to be a part of your life in some way, I have left a gift to my eagle and the others. Once you all are inside, you'll understand why this fireplace was never harmed in the collapse of the castle."

He noticed that she was beginning to fade, and he asked her once more to come back when the birds were there. Instead of answering him, he felt all her love pass though him when she left him, her ghost going through his body.

"Oh, Mother. I have loved you so much. I love you more with each passing day."

He sat there in the hallway and cried for his loss. Yes, he thought to himself, he could understand why she'd not want to hurt her birds like this. It was almost too much for him to bear himself.

Chapter 2

Jude landed on the perch she'd claimed as her own all those centuries ago and looked around. Her eagle, larger than life, could see well beyond what even binoculars could see with a human hand. The waterways looked much like they had all those years ago. Minus, of course, the boats and ships that would be out daily.

The queen had boats too, she only just remembered. They would go out daily with their nets and bring back bounties of fish and other creatures. Turtles were her favorite once she got past the heavy shell. There were other things she remembered too. Things that until this moment had been all but forgotten.

"Hello." She turned slowly and looked at the man before her. She hadn't any idea who he was, and when he approached her perch, he stayed far enough away that she couldn't kill him if he made a sudden move. "I've been awaiting your arrival. If you wish to talk to me, I can understand you as well as Mother did."

"Your mother? I'm afraid I don't know who your mother is, sir." He moved just a little closer to her, and instead of being in front of her now, he was looking out over the turret much as she'd been doing when he spoke to her. "Perhaps if you explained who your mother is, it will jog a memory, and I'll know who you are." There was something about him that touched a memory, but she didn't have it long enough to put a face to who he might be.

"The work on the castle is coming along nicely. It helped me that there was plenty enough magic for me to tap into when I started working." He looked at her. "Do you suppose it would be possible for you to be a woman now? I've enjoyed speaking to you, Judith, but I would also like to see your other half. If you don't mind."

Hopping down to the flat surface of the roofless room, she shifted even before her feet touched the stone beneath her. Keeping her distance from him, just in the event he wanted to harm her, she reached out to any of the other birds to tell them where she was. Mercy told her he was safe. Sure, easy for her to say — she wasn't up in the turret with him.

"Mercy said you are trustworthy. I'm not so sure yet, so I'd keep my distance. I don't have time to fuck around with you today. Besides, I think there is something wrong with you that you're not frightened of my bird. So? What's the matter with you?"

Duncan laughed, and she knew immediately who he was and who his mother was. He laughed like her.

The braying of a jackass. It was much like his mother. She wondered if anyone had pointed that out to him as yet. Not sure what to say to him, she bowed down, so her head was touching the cold stone beneath the two of them.

"Don't do that. Don't bow to me, Judith. Please. We're equals."

She didn't look up at him but wondered what the hell he was talking about. She felt a bit of humor when Mercy asked her if she'd figured it out yet.

I'm fucking pissed off at you. You should have told us. Mercy asked her what fun that would have been. *I wouldn't have landed here in the first place. And secondly, I would have landed on your head to knock some sense into it. What the hell, Mercy?*

When he touched his finger to her chin to lift her head up to his, Jude stared at him. Christ, he looked so much like his mom now that she knew who he was, it was uncanny. The urge to touch him, to see if he was real, had her lifting her hand to his cheek, and his scent hit her — hard.

"No." His lordship nodded as she stood up to back away from him. Every part of her body was at war with the other. Flee or stay? Shift and go, or stand her ground? Whatever happened, she was sure it had to be a joke Mercy was pulling on her. "This can't be right, sire. You're my king. All of our king."

"And you are my queen." She backed up when he moved closer to her. "I'm sorry. I should have said something when I first saw you, but I was told to wait until today. Judith, I've waited for you to be mine all my life, it seems."

"This is supposed to be a joke, right?" He shook his head as more of the conversations with Mercy came to her. "She knew. Mercy knew who you are. She never said a word. I didn't even know that— What is—? You're our king. I'm nothing more than a magical creature."

"No. You're so much more than that, Judith. All of my mother's birds were so much more than just magical creatures. Without you and your sisters, we'd not have this day. The kingdom's people would have perished when the new king arrived, if he was still set to marry my mother. So much—every living thing—is still here because of the six of you. And you are my mate, my other half. My queen." She turned and jumped over the side of the turret. "Judith, come back."

Shifting into her bird, she soared at a height that made her slightly ill. Or was it knowing she had been chosen by someone with a wicked mind to be the lady of the castle? Finding a place to set down, Jude landed on the mountain she'd been to hundreds of times before the death of the queen.

What the hell are you doing? She didn't answer Mercy because, honestly, she had no idea what she was doing. *You can't run away from this, Jude. You have to know he's the perfect person for you.*

You might well have mentioned this before I got here. Mercy told her she wasn't allowed to. *Why? You couldn't have just mentioned that—oh, I don't know, I might find my other half here, and woohoo, he's the king of all the lands we worked for?*

I couldn't tell you, Jude. I couldn't tell anyone. You have no idea how much I wanted to warn you about this. So many times in the last week, I went to just tell you. But I was sworn to secrecy. Jude thought about the many times Mercy had come to her place and hung out with her. *This, you and Duncan coming together, it was foretold by Dante. She knew what her son was to you.*

How did you even figure out she had a son? I didn't know. I'm sure none of the rest of the birds knew about him either. Mercy told her she'd not told them either. *How is it possible she was able to hide not just a baby from us, but her pregnancy as well?*

Duncan was born before she brought us to the castle to change us. Well, that did make sense. *She birthed him after her husband died. Mary — you remember her and her two sons? Well, she raised Duncan as her own, but he's not really hers, and now they're here in the castle together. Even Mary lives here now. If you want, I can send her to you so you can talk to her.*

I don't want to speak to anyone just yet. Lying back on the snowy mountain, Jude wondered at this all coming together. *You said that Dante knew about him and me. How did you find this out?*

The books. And a lot of research. Also, I saw him a couple of times. But once I found it in the books she left for us, I understood a great many things. He's been investing the money that was left for him to care for New Town, and they are living well because of it. The castle, as of the moment I got here and signed it back over to the two of you, has been renovated to this century. Cable, Internet — all the things you'll need to use while being the queen. Jude told her she wasn't going to be a queen. *Honey, I'm sorry to tell you this, but you are. The queen of the lands here,* and everywhere he invested in.

This is all so surreal. Don't you think? Mercy told her that once she'd gotten used to the information, she thought it was the perfect choice. *I don't know how to be a queen. I'm just a bird that is out of sorts.*

You have never been just anything, Jude. There were a lot of times in the past — before I knew what you were, I've come to realize — that you were taking control and getting us on the right road. Times, now that I can look back on them, I realize you were made to be a ruler. Don't you remember all the times we'd be fighting over some investment or where to live? Small things, I know, but all you had to do was point out the flaws in our reasoning, and we'd settle right down. Mercy laughed. *You would never raise your voice like I would have done. You never got angry like Piper would have and burnt us all to a crisp. Jude, you were just there, a calming factor in every single decision we've ever made.*

You're making me sound like a puppy or something. Mercy laughed, and Jude joined her. *I'm guessing right about now his lordship is wondering what the hell he's gotten himself into. I would be. I just left him there.*

Actually, he's here in the room with me. I've not told him that we're speaking. I'm just watching him pace. He does that just like his mother did too. Oh, have you heard his laughter? I nearly fell over when he laughed earlier. She told Mercy she'd figured out who he was by it. *I don't think I'd point that out to him just yet. He's worried he screwed up with you and doesn't know what to do. Miley is about to tell him to fucking find you, by the way. He hasn't been able to fly until now. I think she's also giving him tips on flying. She had to learn a lot, and she's giving him little bits of what she had to learn. I love that kid.*

I do, as well. She's come a long way. Both of you have. Mercy thanked her. *What am I to do? Mercy, I'm not sure I can be a queen to anything or anyone. Do you understand?*

I do, but do you understand that there couldn't have been a better pick to be the queen than you? You're exactly what Dante wasn't. She needed to be who she was to make sure things got done. That we were safe. You don't have to do that. You can rule any way you want and not have to be concerned that the people you rule are going to die from dysentery or starvation. I'm not saying it's going to be easy, but it'll be much less dangerous than it was back when we were made. Yes, there was that, she supposed. *And here is a nice thought you can take to your heart while you're thinking about what to do. He's a generous, handsome man who is exactly like his mother in so many other ways it's almost like he has her spirit within him.*

Jude thought about all the things Mercy had told her. All the things she remembered from when Dante had been alive. She had been a hard ruler, but she'd had to be. Without her making sure everyone pulled their weight and did their jobs, they all would have died.

The trenches around the castle, bringing in water and taking away the waste, were cleaned daily. The water was always fresh when it seeped through the small inlets she had dug for just that reason. She'd been very much in fashion by today's standards, Jude thought. Recycling and up-cycling was a way of life for them all even back then.

Houses would be torn down when it got to the point it

was more repaired than new. The wood was put to other homes if it could be used. What wasn't reusable was burned in fireplaces to keep the homeowners warm. Gardens were recycled in a way that even the left over bushes from the growth would be reused in a way that would thatch roofs, or be dried for pretties to sell. Also, there was the way Dante always knew just how to treat wounds that had festered, how to treat sicknesses that would have killed. Jude now wondered just how much of the future Dante had seen. Obviously enough so she could keep not just the people healthy, but the animals they all depended on as well.

As she sat there, a shadow fell across her, and Jude looked to the sky. At first, she thought it was one of her sisters, but realized it could only be the king. His bird, an eagle like hers, was having trouble staying up. Laughing when a current caught him unawares, she shifted to her bird and joined him in the sky.

I could do this every day. I might be better at it if I did, but this is so lovely. I've never seen the lands as I am right now. No wonder Mother didn't allow her fear of heights to keep her from sailing through the sky like this. Jude told him she had been terrified of falling. *Yes, I still have the harness she wore on one of the birds. Mercy wants to be able to take the children of the village on rides. I told her we couldn't take the children coming on Christmas. I have had enough trouble with the children's home in just getting them out here. Is there anything I can do to convince you that what my mother has done is real?*

I will come around. Eventually. Right now, I'd like to just fly a bit, and not think of the things she might well have done in anticipation of us. She soared high up, then came down at a slow fall, riding the currents as they blew cold wind over the mountain. *The things I love to do as a bird cannot be done in the town where we have all lived. This is a freedom I've not had since we all left here. I can be my original size and not be noticed, but this, right here, this is what I have so enjoyed.*

The two of them flew for what seemed like days. She knew it had been hours since she joined him — the sun setting over the water was a clear sign they'd been out here for so long. Duncan, as he asked her to call him, didn't bring up the fact she was his mate. Thankful for that reprieve, she told him about herself in bits and pieces, as he did the same for her. It was, she supposed, like what had been planned for so long was finally paying off. Or something akin to that.

When they finally landed in the back land of the castle, she shifted to herself almost before touching the earth. Duncan had a bit more trouble with it. Landing, he told her, was a great deal harder than he thought it would be.

It took him three tries to land and shift. The first time he was still much too high to do it and nearly splattered himself all over the snow covered lawn. The second time was much funnier, as he was only partially shifted as he landed. The weight of the large bird on his human legs had her literally rolling in the cold grass as he tried the third time and made it stick.

She was still enjoying herself when he came to stand over her. Putting out his hand to help her up, Jude took it as if he'd been helping her all her life. The magic between them touched her in a way nothing had ever done before.

"I touched your skin earlier and was afraid I'd been wrong about you." She asked him what he meant. "I don't know exactly what I thought, to be honest with you, but I wondered where the punch to my system was. Now, now that we're working on a relationship, I felt it. Did you?"

"Yes. I think I was too afraid to feel much of anything the first time." He didn't let go of her hand, and Jude found she was all right with that—for now. "I'm nervous now too. I don't know what I'm supposed to do with having you as a mate. It's very strange to me."

"Me too. And I've known about it for some time." Jude nodded. "There is some food left for us. I'm afraid we've missed dinner with everyone."

Entering the castle from the rear, Jude had a thought. She'd never been in this part of the castle before. Her only knowledge was of the turrets and the perches Dante had had made for them. Walking into the kitchen, it made her laugh. It was nothing but a kitchen like the one she had in her home now. Telling Duncan her thoughts, she sat down to enjoy a sandwich with him. It was a start, she thought. To what? Well, she thought, time would tell.

~*~

"Who is this again?" Charlie thought he heard someone talking, but right now, all he could hear was static. He hated telephones as much now as he had when the suckers first came out. "Is there anyone there?"

"Grandda?" He nearly fell back when the voice on the other end came through as clear as day. "Grandda? This is Duncan. I'm Dante's son. I was wondering if I could see you."

"Who is this again?" The laughter had him closing his eyes for just a moment. His entire life seemed to pass right before his closed eyes. "I'm sorry, but I've been tricked like this before. You're good, I'll tell you that. But I'm not falling for—"

"I'm standing at the front door. This isn't a trick, and if you'd allow me to come in, you'll never have to worry about collection men again. Nor anything if you'd allow me to take care of you and Grandma. You've no idea how hard I've been looking for you. Mom came to me and told me you were at the cottage. However, when I went there, the place was gone. I'm guessing time took its toll on it. I need to see you, Grandda." With the phone still in his hand, he made his way to the door. It wasn't like it was a long walk—the place they'd been staying at was smaller than some bathrooms he'd been in. "If you open the door, I can help you. I could, I suppose, tell you some things about Mom. Like she was the greatest queen that ever lived. That she was well loved by those around her. She was the greatest mother of all, keeping me safe when others would have kidnapped me to—"

Charlie opened the door. The man standing on the other side didn't move to come into the home he and his missus had been in for the last few years. Nor did he rush him, which was what others had done, trying their best to get something from him to pay down some of the bills the two of them had acquired. He reached for his mate, asking her to come to him.

"Charlie, what are you doing standing there with the door wide open? Are you inviting every bill—? Oh my." He would trust her judgment on this predicament he was currently in. More than anything he'd ever wanted, Charlie wanted this young looking man to be his grandson. Watching her, tearing his eyes from the face he'd thought about for all his life, he watched his lady wife. "Oh my. Duncan? Is it really you?"

"Yes, Grandma, it's really me. I've come to take you home with me." Sara started sobbing then. The years of waiting, of needing someone to say those words to them, had been all they'd wanted. A ghost, he supposed, from their past to come and see them. "I'm so sorry I didn't come here sooner. I didn't know, you see. Mother came to see me a few nights ago and—"

He couldn't wait any longer to have him in his arms. Dragging him to his body, Charlie hugged the boy as tightly as he could manage. He was there—his grandson. Duncan then pulled Sara to him, and the three of them stood there, babbling and bubbling over with tears as their words fell all over each other.

Charlie pulled his handkerchief out of his pocket and rubbed it over his face. He'd always been a proud man, but right now, he just didn't care who saw him sobbing over this. Pulling Duncan all the way into the house, he noticed the beauty standing just outside the door. He put out his hand to pull her in, too, when she spoke to him.

"I loved your daughter more than I ever did anything

in my life. I wanted you to know that." Charlie asked her who she might be. "I'm Jude. Judith Castle. I was one of her birds."

Charlie remembered the birds. The things Dante told him about how they'd saved the castle. He wasn't sure what to say to her. Charlie was aware of them, but not much more. He looked at Duncan when he said her name.

"This is my mate. Judith and I are to be wed—when she says yes, that is. Mom told me long ago I'd be mated to one of her birds. We're just getting to know each other." Charlie asked her if she'd come into the house. "She thinks we should be alone. To catch up on our lives. I could only convince her to come with me, but nothing more."

"Young lady, if you're going to be wedded to my grandson, you're going to be my granddaughter. So you get your bottom in here now so that I can get me a big hug from you. It's been much too— I've not hugged anyone but my missus here in— I sure would appreciate it if you'd come on here and hug this old man. I'm going to get them from the two of you as much as I can from now on." She did as he wanted and hugged him. It occurred to him that she was a delicate little thing, and he pulled back to look at her. "My goodness. You sure are a pretty little bit, aren't you?"

"Thank you."

Sara hugged her next, telling her how glad she was to have met her.

While they were standing there, the door still wide open, a man darkened the doorway. Charlie was embarrassed to have him coming around on a day like this one. This wasn't the time for him to be collecting. Not that he had anything to pay him with anyway. However, before he could open his mouth to run the man off, Judith spoke.

"If you have anything to say to Mr. or Mrs. Beswick, you'll contact their attorney. As of this morning, all their money issues have been taken care of." The man, he didn't know his name, snickered. "Would you like to be laughing out the other side of your face, Mr. Tumble? I'll gladly fix it so you never laugh again without thinking about what I have done to you. I'm not one to fuck with. You'll come to realize that if you don't go away."

"How did you take care of your money issues, Mr. Beswick? Last I heard, just yesterday, as a matter of fact, you didn't have a pot to piss in."

Charlie didn't get a chance to speak to Judith when she told him she was sorry. The movement was nearly too fast for him to have seen properly. The man and his briefcase were just simply gone. Charlie looked at Judith.

"He was annoying. I hope you don't mind, but I've taken care that no one will ever come here again." Charlie nodded at her. "That is if you decide you don't wish to come to the castle and live with Duncan. And myself, I guess. I'd like for you to be there. Both of you."

"Is that man dead?" Judith told him she'd taken care of him, but not killed him. "By taking care of him, I'm assuming I don't want to know what that means."

"I don't mind telling you that he's currently in the middle of his street in front of his house, dancing. I also don't mind telling you that he's buck naked, and tossing dollar bills into the air as he does it." She grinned at him. "I don't think he's going to be collecting on innocent people again either. He was never turning in the money you and Sara gave him."

"I figured he wasn't. Not an honest man, then?" She shook her head. "Do you usually take care of nasty men by making them dance naked in front of their home?"

"No, usually I just kill them. But I didn't want you to think badly of me on our first meeting." He grinned back at her. "You're going to be a lot of fun, aren't you? My sisters, the other birds, they will have a wonderful time teasing you too, I'm thinking."

"I've not had a great deal to be funning about, I think." She told him she was so deeply sorry for that. "You know, I think you mean that. I mean, you're not just mouthing the words because you think I need to hear them, are you?"

"No. I'd never do that to you. Or your wife. But I do want to warn you, I will tell you the truth. So be prepared for it." Charlie stared at the woman. She was someone he could trust. Someone, he thought, he could depend on no matter what was going on. "I will protect you, with my entire being, should you need it. I won't allow anyone to harm or take advantage of you ever again."

"Thank you." He finally closed the door. It was a good feeling, not having to worry about someone barging in on his and Sara's life. Charlie looked around his home, the one he'd been living in for some time now. "I hate it here. It was all we could get into when the cottage fell down around our ears. We didn't know what to do when we heard that our daughter was dead. Felt it like a dagger in our hearts."

"We didn't know you were around, or we, all of us, would have found you sooner. There wasn't anything in the books about you. I think now it was to keep you safe. So no one would come for you to take over the lands and such she'd left behind." Charlie told her he'd thought that was it. "If you come back with us, both of you, you'll be safe. I'd like, and I'm sure the other birds would like to hear of Dante when she was younger. The queen was such a wonderful person. She gave her life for the people in the keep that day. She knew the king of that era would have surely killed her for her lands and monies. Dante decided to go in her own way. But she made sure the people were well beyond the hands of anyone that came around."

Charlie knew his little girl would have done everything in her power to keep people safe. He also knew Dante didn't contact them for the sole reason to keep them out of harm's way. She was and would always be the best part of Sara and himself.

As they joined Sara and Duncan in the little room that served as several rooms at once for them, he sat down on the couch alongside Duncan. He and Sara were talking about the castle. Oh, how he wanted to see it.

"I was just telling Duncan about his mother when she was a child. Even then, she was set on making people's lives better." Charlie agreed and had to smile when his wife continued. "There was this man who lived across the way from us. He'd been down on his luck for some time, and Dante gave him her pin money. But she did it in a way I don't think he realized she'd helped him."

"I have a man much like that one near where we live. He is forever calling me up and telling me that he'll do this or that if someone comes onto his property. I have told him of the six thousand acres that divide us, but he just won't stop. I think he's a lonely man who needs to talk to someone. I give him that." Judith told Duncan she'd take care of him. Charlie's mind jumped to where Duncan's went, and he asked her not to kill him. "I think, as I said, he's lonely."

"I wasn't going to murder him. I was just going to talk to him." She looked at him, and Charlie felt his face heat up from her look. "I'm not a monster. Unless, of course, he needs his ass kicked. Then all bets are off. I've not had a tasty meal as my bird in a long time."

He wasn't sure if she was joking or not. Charlie wasn't even sure if she had a sense of humor. But when she winked at him with a devilish smile, he knew he was never going to play any kind of betting game with her. He'd not just lose his clothing, but she might well make him dance in the street naked himself.

Chapter 3

Jude was trying her best to remain calm. Since the first time she realized what he was to her, Duncan had been right there. It didn't matter if she was just going into or coming out of the bathroom, he was standing just outside the door. If he didn't leave her alone to give her time to think, she was going to be a widow before she ever claimed her mate.

"Do you need anything?"

No, she told him, then stopped walking to the kitchen. He ran into her from behind. Okay, she thought, I've had enough. She turned toward him and let go of her temper. "Go the fuck away. I mean it. You're too close. Too much. Just leave me to think, or I swear to you, I'll take flight and leave you here on the ground."

"I'd find you." She growled at him and desperately wanted to hit him. But he didn't seem to be bothered by her anger or her telling him to go away. "I'd like a kiss. If you think you can give me one without taking my lips off."

"I might well yet do that." He simply grinned larger at her. "Look. You're driving me insane. I'm not usually so closely followed when I'm working. I want to make things absolutely perfect for the party. I can't get shit done if you're right on my fucking heels all the time."

"You kiss me, and I'll leave you alone for a little while." She asked him how long was a little while. "Good question. Thirty minutes. I'll leave you alone for thirty minutes, then come back for another payment. I think that's a fair trade. Don't you?"

"No. A fair trade would be me having Piper blow her breath over you and ending everything that is bothering me." Duncan told her Piper would not do it; she liked him. "Not as much as she does me. Now, one kiss, and you're going to go and find yourself something to do that does not involve walking all over me when I stop."

As soon as he pulled her into his arms, she knew this was a mistake. He was going to take so much more from her than just a kiss. Which, she thought, was going to be nothing like a touching of the lips. Wrapping her arms around him as he bent her to his body, Jude felt the warning signals go off everywhere in her mind.

"Judith, I've loved you all my life."

His mouth grazed over hers, the barest of touches. The heat was there, along with so much passion, she was almost giddy for him to taste her. As his lips hovered over hers for a scant second, just enough for her to want to beg him to kiss her, he took her lips with his, and Judith knew she was never going to get enough of this man.

The kiss stole her breath. It made her heart skip several beats as he held her to him. Needing something to hold on to, she curled her fingers into his hair. Held onto any part of him she could hold. She felt his tongue, all but begging for entrance. Not only did she allow him in, but welcomed him with her own.

Nothing in this world or any other could have prepared her for the devastation his mouth did to her body. Even when he lifted his head, just for the briefest of moments, Jude wanted more. Needed more of anything he was willing to give her. As he dipped his head, taking her mouth once again, she felt the air move around her, the ground beneath her feet shift. Jude thought for sure his kiss had ended all life as they knew it.

The second kiss was everything. Jude felt her body tighten with a climax. The kiss taking her to peak was scary when she thought of what he'd do to her when they made love. Duncan lifted his head once again and held her to him while she got herself under control. Telling her heart it was all right for it to continue to beat while inhaling slowly, she felt Duncan set her up on her feet and hold her. Her nostrils filled with not only his scent but the smell of her own lust as well.

"Are you all right?" She couldn't answer him, so she simply shook her head. "Yes, I think I feel the same way. I didn't expect—I suppose I should have guessed it would be wonderful to taste of you, but I never thought the world would move for us."

"I came." As soon as the words left her mouth, she was mortified by them. But he didn't tease her or even laugh at her. Instead, he leaned his forehead to hers and held her upright. "I'm not sure what I should be saying to you right now."

"I don't either, to be honest. I never thought a kiss could do so much to one's body. I know I've never felt this way with anyone before." She told him she'd not either. "I don't want to allow you to walk away from me. I have a feeling, and I have no idea why, but if you walk away from me right now, I'm going to think this was all a dream."

She pinched him, taking a chunk of the flesh on his arm and twisting it hard. When he asked her what she was doing, she smiled at him.

"I was making sure we were neither one dreaming." He looked at her with furrowed brows. Jude wondered if he hadn't thought it was funny. Then, he did the most incredible thing—he threw back his head and laughed. It was just like hearing his mother laughing at some joke decades ago. "Your mother laughed like that. She never cared what people thought of her when she was in good humor. And she was a great deal—in good humor."

"When she'd come to visit me, Mom would always have a tale about you and the other birds. How Mercy would take her up too high in the sky. How easily you were able to take down a kingdom. She loved you six like her own children, I think." Jude told him she had loved Dante just as much. "She knew that, as well. Mom, she told me once that without you birds there with her, she would never have survived life. Living to be as old as she did, it wasn't something that common to women of that era."

Jude made her way to the gift room. It was actually the living room, but the furniture had all been put in storage, and gifts for the children had been brought in. The large bags, filled with several gifts, had a name on each of them. Jude was glad when Duncan joined her in the room. It didn't even bother her when he was close to her any longer.

"Before I forget to tell you, I've spoken to your neighbor, Mr. Bloom. And before you ask, yes, he's still alive." Duncan asked her what he wanted now. "I'm sending a car for him to be here in the morning when the children arrive. I told him we needed someone here to tell the children the Christmas story. I appealed to his sense of duty in making sure it was done correctly. I also know this will be his last holiday. He isn't long for this world."

"Does he know?" Jude told him what she'd found out. "So you have the gift of seeing as well. I do, but it is sort of temperamental on what it shows me."

"Mine is much stronger since I came here." She turned her back to him as she continued. "I know too that you and I are going to have a child by the next Christmas. It's not of our body."

"I don't have a problem with that if you don't." Jude told him she didn't care so long as he knew she knew nothing of small children. "I know a little. For a while, I was a children's doctor. I know seeing them as a doctor isn't the best of circumstances, but I did learn a great deal. What do you think of my grandparents living here?"

The change of subject didn't bother her—it was the question. Turning to look at him, she wondered why he'd think she would have a problem with them living in his home. When she told him what she thought, he shook his head.

"No, it's our home. I did this for us. All the improvements were done with you in mind. The perches have been put back the way they were simply for us to use when we fly. This house, that's all it is—just a house. I want to make it a home with you. It seems silly to say this, but I've never lived in my own home before. I've lived in other people's homes, lived with people in a big house. But never have I lived in my own home before."

Jude thought about what he was saying. She hadn't either. It had either been a small place where she could store things, a place so people wouldn't be asking questions about where she lived when she was out. And if it hadn't been just a place for others to see and know about, she'd lived with the other birds.

"I don't know much about having a home either. I've seen the houses that Mercy and Blaze have. I think their mates have a great deal to do with the touches I can see there now. But as for making myself a nest, a home, I've never had the inclination to have one before." Jude sat down on the floor to finish up the last of the candy canes she'd been putting on each of the smaller packages for the adults coming in the morning. "This is our first Christmas too. I mean, we've celebrated them, but nothing like this. I can't remember the last time I put up a tree or got a card from someone." She thought of all the times she'd not even realized it was the holidays until it was almost too late.

"I think we're in the same mind frame on that. You've been around for so long, it became just another day to you. Another year you've been alive. My grandparents have been doing the day to day for a long time, Grandma told me. Just getting through one day at a time." Jude asked him about their money situation. "I didn't know about it. I'm glad you were able to take care of all those outstanding debts. I would have gotten in touch with them before had I thought they were still alive."

"I can understand why Dante didn't tell anyone about them. They would have been murdered to bring her to heel. It was like her hiding you away. If they didn't know about you, you couldn't be harmed in any way and used against her. They would have too." Duncan told her he knew that too. "I don't know why she didn't tell us about you, however. I'm sure she had her reasons. Maybe she was afraid if someone were to capture us, or worse yet, if she were to fall to another king, we'd have to tell them about you. I wouldn't have. But back then, we were simply her birds and not anything that could have changed into a human form."

"In one of her books, she talks about changing you to humans when she was in a place she could live without the help. I don't think she meant to make it so you could be birds too. But when she spoke of you six, she seemed to have hated what she'd done to you. Making you larger than life. Her own death squad, so to speak." Duncan sat on the floor with her, tying the ribbon around some of the packages as she was doing with the candy canes. When he stood up suddenly and smacked his hand on his head, she thought for sure something had happened. "The fireplace. I completely forgot to show it to you guys. Can you round up the others for me? Mom showed me something in the fireplace that I had to give to you. I cannot believe I forgot about it. I'll meet you in the living room with them."

When he took off toward the back of the house, Jude did what he asked. *He said his mother told him about a place in the fireplace we have to look at.* Mercy asked if she could bring Miley too. *I don't know why not. I mean, she's a part of us as much as Joel is. But I don't know what he's talking about, just so you know, so I can't give you a heads up on what might be in the fireplace. I don't even know if it's going to be dangerous. Not that I think she'd want to hurt us after all this time.*

When the others showed up in the living room, Jude asked to have something brought in to tide them over until dinner. They were eating later tonight, so they could go to bed full and get up early. She had no idea why that made them all sleep better, to have a full belly. But it worked, and she wasn't going to change it now.

Grandma and Grandpa Beswick came into the room with them. Jude had asked them to be there as well. Tomorrow they were going to get their titles back, and Jude was excited about that. They'd be Lord and Lady Beswick of Honeysuckle Estates, the name of their estate long ago. They'd have their own home if they wanted to move, but she and Duncan hoped they'd live in the castle with them.

The two of them were sweet, and she was getting to love everything about them being there.

~*~

Duncan tried to remember which of the stones his mother had told him to push. If he was honest with the others in the room, he was nervous about doing this. Before he could settle on one stone, like it was going to make a difference if it was the wrong one, Joel stopped him.

"Before you do that, I'd like to say something." Duncan turned and nodded when he stood up. "I've only been a part of this family for a short time. I wanted to tell all of you how much I've come to love you. I know it's sappy, but I had to say it. You know, just in case there is some kind of poison in there that's going to kill us all off." Mercy told him he was immortal, and he didn't have to worry about that. "Oh yeah. Well, hell, go ahead and release the Kraken."

Duncan was still laughing when he pushed the correct stone. Standing back out of the way when the rest of the chimney started to move, he watched the entire thing open up and show an entire room in the back of the thing.

It was a huge opening once the fireplace moved back and out of the way. The room seemed to light its way deep inside before it started to illuminate the area where they were standing. When he looked deeper into the room, he noticed it wasn't a room at all but a long corridor. There were steps that went both up and down from where they were standing. The stone, which was what it was made of, looked like it was one continuous stone that just naturally conformed to the shape it was now in.

"Now what?" He told Bryson he didn't know. "Do we go up, or should some of us take different stairs? I mean, it's sort of a long looking way up or down, don't you think?"

"Up." Duncan nodded when Jude told him up was the way to go. "I think if we were meant to go down, it would have told us so. But up.... I have no idea why, but that seems like where we should begin. Don't you think?"

They couldn't go up the flight of stairs in pairs because the stairs were narrow but sturdy. As he led the way up, he could see there were torches above his head that lit the areas as they got closer to it. When he was ready to have a seat and rest, he saw the floor leveling out just as he cleared the last few steps.

"Oh, Mother." The room, for this was a room, expanded by magic as he stood looking around. The others came into the room, and it grew again, making the room look as large as the living room they'd only just left. But it was nothing like a living room with the items that were in the place. "Look, Mercy, this has your name on it. There are trunks with each of our names on them. Including Miley."

Piper started laughing, and he asked her what she'd found. "It's a trunk for my mate. It hasn't a name on it, but it says, 'to the man who loves my bird, Piper.' I wonder what this could be? Surely it's not money, do you think?"

As soon as Esme touched her fingers to the box that had her name on it, it disappeared. The note under it explained the trunk was now in her room in the house. So they'd not have to carry them down, Duncan supposed. Each of them did the same, touching just a finger to the top of the trunk so it too would be in their room. The trunks, however, were not the only things in the room.

There were pieces of art covered in waxed cloth — sacks of seeds with the names and how to grow them on each bag. Duncan handed Miley a sack that had her name on it, and she laughed when she poured the gems, all of them worth a fortune, into her hand. There was an entire wall with swords leaning against it. They, too, were wrapped up in cloth with their bejeweled pummels showing.

"How do you suppose she was able to stash all this here? It must have taken her years to do this." Joel picked up one of the larger handwoven baskets and saw it was filled with saplings. Trees he was sure no one had seen in centuries. "How does this even work? I mean, to look at these, you'd think they were only just pulled from the ground. But they've been in here for at least as long as Dante has been gone. Your mother, she must have been more powerful than we even guessed her to be."

"I think you're right." Duncan looked at the unframed paintings that leaned against one of the other walls. "I know some of these artists. They were here and gone long after Mom died. How did she do that?"

"She wanted you to have a nest egg." Grandma picked up a smallish trunk that had her name on it, and Duncan was glad she'd thought of her parents too. "Oh, Charlie. Look. They're our eggs. The ones we had to sell off when it was needed. All my little eggs."

They were beautiful too. Each egg was handmade,

the opening covered in gold and diamonds. There were a dozen or so in the chest she had, and Grandda opened his to show the rest they'd had at one time. Duncan felt his eyes fill with tears at how his mother had taken care of them all, even after all this time. But what he wouldn't give to have her there with them today.

The room's contents emptied to their separate bedrooms as they touched each of the pieces. He noticed that Miley had somehow found herself a cane covered in gems and stones. Some of the things, like the crates of eggs, were sent along too after his grandparents put them on the floor. As he was making his way to the lower levels of the magical place, he wondered why his mom hadn't just put it away someplace they could all have it. As soon as he stepped into the very lower level of the hidden rooms, he understood everything.

There in the corner was the very thing he'd been hunting for since he'd started working on the castle, what he thought was his mother's jewels. There were a great deal of them too. More than he thought there would have been. Mercy took a look at it and smiled at him.

"It's from the raids we were on. She never said what she was doing with the jewels we took. Being birds then, I guess it never occurred to us to ask. But this is it, all of it, I'm sure. Not only is it the jewels, Duncan, but I'm sure if we were to look around a little more, we'd find all the stash from all the raids we were on. She's hoarded it for all of us. Your mom, she was a gem of all gems if you ask me. I miss her more every day."

There weren't names on things here. It was just piled up, some of the piles as tall as he was. Gold coins, too, spilled out of the trunks they were in and onto the floor. The sparkle of diamonds made the room bright—gems of all kinds laid in large pools of like gems. There was silver too, dinnerware sets of it, and urns that seemed to be full of other things, such as chain mail and gloves for jousting. He thought it funny to find his mother's armor, standing tall in the corner of the room. Duncan wondered what they were to do with such a bounty when his grandda spoke up.

"You're going to have to bring this out a little at a time, I'm thinking. If you hit the market with all this, nothing will be worth anything. Just a little of it at a time should keep the market high. As for what to do with it, I'm sure it will be told to us. Dante, she would have had a plan and a place for this all." Grandda nodded at him and smiled. "I knew my girl was going to save us all. Didn't you?"

"I knew too." He looked for Judith, who was sitting on one of the ugliest chairs he'd ever seen, reading something. Going to her, he took the book she handed him and knew it was his mother's handwriting. He read only a couple of lines before he cleared his throat to speak. "She said she would like for you all to live here. Not in the castle, she goes on to explain, but here on the land."

"Dante said she wanted her family here, all of us so that she can rest in peace. It's her wish too that we take the bounty here in this room and make sure it's used for goodness. The people who had hoarded this much wealth didn't use it for anything but taking up space in their castle." Jude stood up and went to his grandda. "There is a message in the book for you as well. She said to tell you that you and her mom were forever in her heart and that had she been able to, she would have made sure you were forever taken care of. She is sorry from the bottom of her heart that it came to the point you were in before someone could rescue you. But it was more important for her to have you live out your life with her son and her birds than anything else she could have done for you."

Grandda blew his nose and thanked Jude for that. After he hugged her, Grandda went to stand with Grandma. Duncan was thrilled to be able to have them here with him. Now he just hoped he could convince the others to stay close too.

The things in the lower level were left there for now. He wasn't sure what they could do with the seeds and saplings she'd left for them at this time of year, so they all agreed it would be the perfect place to keep them. The other things, the trunks from the upper level, would be gone through too after tomorrow. It was exciting to him just to think how much his mother had done for everyone before she passed away. Duncan couldn't stop wishing she was here with them right now. It would have been the most perfect holiday ever, he thought. Not just for him, but for everyone here.

At dinner, he decided to try and see what the thought was on having everyone move here. There was plenty of room for as much space as any of them wanted. Good schools and he'd been able to put in a landing strip when he'd purchased his jet a few years ago. Everything a family would need was right here. Standing up when they were all seated, he cleared his throat to have his say. Before he was able to even say the first word, Mercy cut him off.

"Yes, we'll stay if that was what you were working up to ask us. We've all been talking it over since we arrived here. We realized from the very first day that we needed to be here where our magic is stronger. We also understand you'll have to have Jude here, as your mate. All of us decided that we, too, would love to live here with everyone close by." Mercy winked at him. "Also, you should know we've taken a vote, and we're all right with you being king."

"Well, thank you so very much." They all laughed, and so did Duncan. "I'm happy to hear you'll be staying. It's been wonderful for me to have you all close to hear about my mom in a way I'd never been privy to before. I thank you for that. My mom was...I miss her every day, but with all of you here, it's been more bearable, less lonely, and easier to see why she gave up her life so that the six of you could go on and do her work for her. I thank you for that."

When he sat down, he felt, for the first time, what it was like to have a family. It had only been him and Mary and her son for so long he didn't know what to expect when the others arrived. Now, having them here, it was as if it was supposed to be like this. Loud. Fun and loving. Yes, Duncan thought, his mother had had the right idea when she'd told them to all live here. They would depend and lean on each other when necessary. But for the most part, they'd be happy.

By the time he was ready for some downtime, having never had to sleep before, Duncan wished all of them a good night as they went to the upper floors to their bedchambers. There were a few things he still wanted to take care of. Mostly it was to plot out the land surrounding the castle. Somehow he knew they'd want to be here, but not close. Privacy was something he depended on as well.

Entering the room, Duncan was surprised to find Judith still in the living room working on a couple of more packages when he went in to turn off the tree for the morning. Seeing her on the floor, leaning against the couch, all he could think about was that he belonged to her. When she turned to look at him, her eyes bright with happiness, Duncan made his way to her without, he was sure, touching the floor once.

Chapter 4

"I'm in love with you." Duncan didn't say anything back, and Jude felt her temper snap. "When someone says that to you, Duncan, you should at least acknowledge it in some way. Not sit there like a bump on—"

"I love you. I was, in my own way, trying to figure out a way to say it so it would be the most romantic thing you've ever heard." She grinned at him and told him saying it at all was romantic to her. "Then I love you to the moon and back. I love you more than there are stars in the sky. I love you with every beat my heart makes, every drop of blood that runs in my body."

"That was perfect." She leaned back against the couch again, looking up at the tree. "This is beautiful. I've said it before, I know, but with the house quiet, the tree here lit up like it is, it's so nice. I know I'd get bored with it sooner rather than later, but there are times when I would love to have the tree up all the time. Just for moments like this one.

Will you make love to me?"

"No. I'd rather we made love to each other." Jude turned her head, just enough to look at Duncan. "What are you thinking right now? I'd like to know you better."

"I'm not thinking about much of anything, really. Just marveling how much I've come to love being in the castle. Knowing too, I guess, that the others are going to be close enough to speak to. To visit. Miley and I have a good relationship too. I think, sometimes, that I'd love to skip over having an infant and having a child her age. However, I'm guessing that not all children are like her at her age." Duncan told her it was doubtful any child was like Miley at any age. "You might be correct on that too. She's a delight."

"She keeps Mercy in check too." That was true. Mercy seemed to be calmer and nicer when Miley was in the room. "I have a bed for us. It was one of the ones in storage I had brought here. The mattress arrived just before you and the others joined me here. Would you like to go up?"

"No. I'd like for you to make love to me right here. Under the tree." He moved closer to her. "You're all right with it? Making love right here in the room where everyone is going to be in a few hours? Now that I think on it, I think—"

"Don't think. Just feel." He kissed her then, taking her breath away with his mouth. He looked down at her from his position on the floor and smiled. "You're so beautiful, I think seeing you naked and in my arms is going to be just too much for me and my poor little heart."

He asked her not to undress herself. She was all right

with him stripping her things off. It was like an unveiling to her, like he was opening a much anticipated gift. She supposed in a way, that was just what he was doing, opening her up so that the two of them could be together.

Duncan pulled her up from the floor as he began his work on disrobing her. Touching her fingers to his skin was so wonderfully sexy. It was soft yet firm. Duncan worked hard every day, and it showed in the way his body had formed. When she was naked before him, he didn't touch her but took his fill of looking at her.

"I was wrong about how wonderful you'd look to me for the first time. I don't think there have been words invented that convey how lovely you are. How wonderfully beautiful you look." Jude told him she loved him. "And I you, Judith. I love you with all my heart."

They didn't make love so much as they touched one another. Familiarized themselves with the other's body. She found out that he was ticklish along his ribs. That his nipples were hard peaks, as were hers. His body was smooth except for the line of fur that went from his navel to his cock. His cock, she saw, was dark with blood, and as stiff as her own nipples.

"I would love to make love to you slowly, to taste every inch of you. But the way you're looking at me has me wanting to fill you right now. To come deep inside of you so that I might claim you." Jude wrapped her hand around his cock. "Christ, Judith. That's not helping at all."

"I want to take you into my mouth." His groan made her pussy heat. "There is so much about you I want to explore. Things I want to taste of you. Touch too."

"I'm at your disposal. Do with me as you wish, love." He smiled devilishly. "But know I'm going to want to be able to do the same things to you when you're finished. If I survive you, that is."

Being able to explore him was amazing. She could touch him anywhere she wanted, which she did. His spine was sexy to her, the way it started at his head, and ended in his wonderfully firm ass. When she went to her knees, he begged her to touch his cock. Licking his knees, fondling his calves, nearly got her into deep trouble with him.

"I'm going to come all over you if you don't touch me soon. I swear I'm going to explode right— Holy mother of god, yes."

Taking his cock into her mouth, she tasted the salty flavor of his precum. The warmth of it was amazing, and Jude decided she needed more. Swallowing around him had Duncan grabbing her hair and holding her still. The more he fucked her mouth, the more of his essence filled her.

The way he was fucking her mouth made her own pussy wet with need. Touching herself, she nearly came apart when her fingers brushed over her sensitive nub. She wanted more, needed to come like this, and touched herself once again.

Coming like this was like nothing she'd ever done before. Jude had had sex before, but she was just coming to realize that was all it had been—sex. This was so much more. Looking up at Duncan had her moaning. He was more than just handsome — he was everything she'd ever thought about in a man, and more.

Duncan pulled back; his cock made a delicate popping noise when he pulled from her mouth. Him jerking her up from the floor and bending her over the couch wasn't what she had expected. As soon as he slammed his cock deep into her pussy, she came so hard that stars danced in front of her closed eyes. Her body stiffened with it as a loud scream seemed to come from her very core.

When Duncan leaned over her, nearly taking her to the seat, he told her to come again. The need to fulfill his command was so powerful it took her breath away when she inhaled sharply. The primal sound of his voice, the way his body seemed to become thicker, larger than life, gave her all she needed to come again, this time with him.

There were more than stars this time. She could see rainbows and ribbons. Birds in flight, colored fireworks that seemed to go on forever. Just when she thought she could take no more, Duncan told her to come again. Her body, in tune with his, not only brought her to peak once again, but every part of her seemed to collapse at the finish, and she welcomed the darkness that took her with open arms.

Jude woke suddenly and realized she was no longer on the floor. The bed she was in was firm enough that she knew she'd get a good night's sleep no matter what she'd done during the day. Reaching for Duncan, hoping he'd be there beside her, she was sad to find his side of the bed not only empty but cold as well. Then he spoke to her from across the room.

"I love you so very much, Judith." She asked him why he was way over by the fireplace. "I was afraid of waking you, and I've enjoyed watching you sleep. You don't snore. I have no idea why that seemed important to tell you."

"I guess we'll have to wait to find out if you do or not." Duncan explained to her that he never slept. "Really? When I woke just now, I was thinking I could sleep in this bed and get a very refreshing night's sleep. You don't sleep at all?"

"I don't. Mom didn't either. I only found that out recently when I was going over her journals. She mentioned that you would need it, especially when the children arrive. I didn't read too much into that, thinking we'd both need to rest when we have children." She asked him again why he was over by the fireplace. "No reason other than I did enjoy watching you in your slumber. You're very selfish of space, I've noticed as well."

"I've never shared my bed with a person overnight before." He thanked her for that. "It's very strange, but I feel as if I've gotten a full night's rest right now. Like I could get up and be productive if I wanted to."

"We have only a couple of hours before our guests arrive. I have several questions I'd like to ask of you." She dressed herself in warm clothing and moved to the fireplace to start a fire. "Ah, yes, that feels wonderful. I can do that as well, light a fire with only a touch. Would you like to adopt any of the children we have coming today? Several of them are older than the majority of them coming. They have, I've been told, given up on having a home and parents for themselves."

"Not that it matters, but why haven't they been adopted before now? I'm asking because it's been my experience that people toss away children that don't conform to something they have in their heads." Duncan pulled her to him, and she sat on his lap as he told her he knew that as well. "I've never really thought about having children, but I think I'd want a brood of them. I don't think I'd care if they were from my body or not. I think, and I know this is just as true as it was when I was just starting out as a human, children don't need parents as much as they need guidance. Most of the older children have no one to tell them right from wrong. Or so it seems."

"Your question as to what is wrong that they've not been adopted before now—I actually know the reason. When I set this up, the managers of the place the children are coming from had decided, quite on their own, that we'd not want the older children to come around. They're nine and sixteen now, a boy and a girl. Anyway, she told me like it was going to be a problem for me as well. Apparently, their parents had been put in prison for robbing a bank. I think she somehow believes them to be tainted in some way by what their parents did." Jude told him that it hadn't tainted him to have a bastard of a father. "No. I told her the same thing. I don't think she particularly cares for me except for the money I donate there."

"Yes, well, I think we both know money speaks volumes to that sort of people and their mindset. When can they move in with us?" Duncan laughed and kissed her on the nose. "In the event you didn't know, that wasn't really an answer."

"I'll have the rooms set up for them when they arrive." He looked at the clock on the dresser. "In about three hours. How about we figure out what we want in the way of rooms for them, such beds and the like, and let them decide what it is they want for the rest of the things we get for them?" Jude asked him if there were stores open she didn't know about. "Not that I'm aware of. But I have the same magic as my mother, I believe. I can visualize a room, and it fills out the way I see it. I'm sure you might well have it too. Try it out in this room."

"No. Not this room. As far as I'm concerned, this room is off-limits to changing around." Duncan asked her why this room. "Our bedroom should be just the way we leave it. I want that much in the way of comfort. I want to know it will be the same as we left it. Sort of...I guess you could call a security blanket kind of thing."

Duncan agreed with her, and she was glad. Being able to mess around with the rest of the castle was going to be fun. But just as she said to him, she wanted the comfort of having things where she left them in this room, even if it was just leaving a towel on the floor and it being there when she returned.

They were headed downstairs when Duncan told her more about the kids. The boy, Abraham — Abe for short — was tested for autism. He wasn't autistic, just shy. The young girl, sixteen, had been watching over her brother since he was born. Duncan told her he thought that might

be another reason for the two of them not being adopted —
they came as a pair. No one, it seemed to him, wanted them
both. But he hoped the two of them would.

"Of course we'll take them both. What a thing to
wonder about. They need each other as much as the two
of us do. I can't believe anyone would ever think it was all
right to separate the two of them." Duncan took her hand
into his and kissed the back of it as they entered the kitchen.
"I don't cook. I can if I really have to, but I don't do kitchen
work well at all."

"We have Meridiam here as a first-rate cook." Duncan
introduced her as his queen. Meridiam curtsied to her, then
smiled at Duncan. "We'd like a little something light if you
have time, please. The children should be here soon. I'm
sure you have it all under control in here?"

"It is, sire. The food is ready to go out as soon as they're
in the castle. It's all been prepared by the little people."
Duncan explained to Jude that they had several faeries
working for the house. "I hope you don't mind, miss, but I
use them in here on nights you will entertain."

"I'm all for making anything you need there for you.
I want you to want to cook for us, and if you need them
here full time, I'm sure we can work out something to make
that happen for you as well." Meridiam smiled at her. "You
tell me what it is you want or need, and I personally will
get it for you. I love to eat, and I eat a great deal. There is
extraordinarily little that I won't eat, but we'll go over that
when it's less of a busy morning for us all. Okay?"

"Yes, miss. And I thank you for that. It would be nice

to have a staff here to do the everyday things. If you'd not mind, I can take care of the hiring of them for us." Jude told her whatever she needed. "Thank you again. It's just like the good king here said — you have your heart in the right place and want things to go smoothly."

Jude enjoyed the conversation as she ate her warm scones. She especially liked the seeds and nuts her bird would enjoy. With the nice hot cup of tea she had with two scones, Jude was able to meet the faeries that would be working in the kitchen with Meridiam. There would be others hired for the rest of the household when the new year was coming in. Jude was as excited as she'd ever been for the children to arrive.

"They're here."

Everyone gathered in the front hall. As soon as the first two people — the adults, she assumed — got off the bus, she knew there was going to be trouble. When Mercy grabbed her hand, she looked at her.

"Let me handle this. I want to." She asked her if she knew what had happened. "Yes. If you allow me to take care of it, then it will be all right. However, I might have to hurt that bitch standing there."

"You do what you have to do. I'm not sure what is going on, but I won't have one person fuck this up for the kids." Mercy said she'd make it right. "Thank you."

~*~

Tracy wasn't sure what was going on but moved into the hallway where the noise was coming from. She and her brother had been left behind this morning. Ms. Holloway had said they'd done something wrong and would be dealt with when she returned. No amount of begging would get her to tell them what they'd done to make it so her brother could at least go to the Christmas party without her. The woman standing in the hall looked directly at her when she asked what was wrong.

"Are you Tracy Jamie?" She nodded, still unsure what the guard, Mad Max, everyone called him, was doing in front of Abe's room. "I want you to get yourself ready to go with me. Also, your brother, if you please. You're coming to the party even if I have to murder someone to have you there."

Tracy started forward, her mind set on going to make sure Abe was all right. He'd been locked away from her when Ms. Bitch left. It was what Tracy called her behind her back every time she had to deal with her.

"Your brother is fine, I promise. Get your things gathered up. Everything. And I'll do the same for Abe." Tracy told her she didn't have much. "You know what, just leave it all. Whatever you need once we're at the castle, I'm sure we can get it for you. This man here, he is going to walk away from me and live to see another day."

"We've been told we can't attend the party." The woman told her she knew better. "I have to live here, miss. They'll kick us out, and I don't know if I can care for my brother on the streets. He's all I have in the world."

"Of course you care for him. Trust me when I tell you you're both going to be fine. I swear it on my unborn child here, you both are going to be fine. Get your brother, and we'll be set to go." Mad Max told the woman they weren't going anywhere without the permission of the headmistress. "You will walk away now and not try and stop us. Go to your room and sit there. Wait. You'll tell me now why the two children here were not allowed to go to the party."

"Ms. H., she don't like them none. She believes them to be a wart on her good works." She asked him if he thought that too. "I don't think much—she told me not to. They didn't do nothing but be in her way, she tells me. But I was to have me some of the girl, if I wanted, in payment for not letting them go to the party."

The man fell back. It wasn't until the woman looked at her bloodied knuckles that Tracy understood she'd hit him. When she looked at her, Tracy took a step back. She didn't want to be hurt or raped by anyone today.

"I swear to you, I would never harm you. My name is Mercy Oliver. I have a daughter about your age who was really looking forward to you and your brother coming today." Tracy told her again how she needed to live here for her brother. "I didn't want to tell you this, but the man and his wife who are having this party for you guys are going to take you in as their own. If you don't trust what I'm saying to you, I'll call Jude right now, and she will verify it. Jude is my sister."

"You swear nothing will happen to Abe? I can take it, but it hurts his heart when someone yells at him. He's very shy." Tracy looked at her brother's door and the chain that was over the doorway. "She does this to him when he won't participate in classroom work or speak when she tells him to. He doesn't care for her."

"No one does, I'm thinking. Come on, honey. Let's get you and your brother fixed up, and we'll be on our way." Nodding, she started for the keys on Mad Max's belt. Tracy watched as not only the chains fell away, but the door disappeared too. Tracy asked if she'd done that. "I did. To chain anyone in a room isn't right. But what she's done to this young man is going to get her in deep shit if I have anything to do about it."

"Will you? Have anything to do with it, I mean?" Abe was in the corner, his head covered with the thin blanket he'd been allowed. "Come on, Abe. We're going to the party. Do you want to see what kind of food they have? I bet they even have ice cream for us." He looked at her while she calmly told Mercy what had him so afraid. "They chain him to the bed at night. I have tried to keep them from doing it to him, but they chain me up too. I can't help him if they do that to both of us."

"Come along." She could hear the anger in Mercy's voice, but never once did she raise her voice while speaking to her or Abe. "I have to make one stop on the way out, but my husband, his name is Joel, is out there waiting for you at the car. He is a genuinely nice man. Get in the car, and I'll be out shortly."

"Don't do anything stupid." Mercy looked at her, the anger seemingly clearing from her eyes. "Don't do whatever you're thinking about. This place might be run like shit, but it's all a lot of these kids have—other than sleeping on the streets. Promise me you won't do whatever it is you think needs to be done, and we'll head to the car without any trouble."

"Do you have any idea what she's doing here?" Tracy took a big chance and nodded. No one knew as much as she did about this place, other than the bitch. "All right. I won't do anything right now. But you have to promise me to speak with Jude when you can. Not today — today is for fun. But soon after the other children leave. Promise me that, Tracy, and I'll do as you asked."

"I swear to you on my brother's life, I will tell her everything she needs to get this place under new management. It will be the truth as I know it." Mercy stared at her for another few seconds before nodding and following her and Abe out. "Thank you for trusting me."

Joel was just where Mercy had said he'd be. He didn't try and shove Abe into the car but allowed him to move at his own pace. When he stood in front of the front door of the big limo, Joel not only opened it for him to sit inside, but he also asked if he'd allow him to buckle him in. It was the first time Abe had allowed anyone to do anything for him but her. She knew at that moment she could not only trust these people, but she thought she might be able to get them to take care of Abe as he needed to be.

"I'm going to be eighteen in a year and a half. I know people are only looking for babies. So if you have any pull with the couple you said is going to take us, I'd like for you to see if they'll allow me to stay until I can get my brother situated." Mercy asked her why she thought they'd turn her out when she turned eighteen. "As I said, people looking for children don't want a grown woman hanging around too."

"I think you're going to be pleasantly surprised by Jude and Duncan. They're as good a couple as that bitch isn't." They both heard laughter from the front seat, and Tracy knew it was her brother. "He's had some trauma in his life, hasn't he? Someone hurt him badly."

"Yes." She looked out the window as the houses became fewer and fewer, and the open fields became more. "His father did it. Not to him directly, but he sold him to one of his buddies. His mom thought it was a hoot. He has nightmares about it, and I got the information from him when I woke him from a bad dream."

"Does he visit them?" Tracy said he'd not seen them since they'd been arrested. "Do you think he'd want anything to do with them?"

"No. Why?" Mercy didn't say anything, but Joel did. He asked her if he would be happy if they were gone. "You mean dead? I doubt very much he's given much thought about them being around him very much. I'm sure he couldn't care less if they were alive or dead. However, I don't want you to do it. You're very ready to right wrongs with killing, aren't you?"

"In this, selling that young man to other men is a killing offense if you ask me. No one, especially a parent, should ever have something like that even enter their head about their own flesh and blood. Do you?" Tracy didn't, but she didn't want this woman to have it on her conscience that she'd killed someone. "Killing them won't ever be on my mind after they're gone. People like them make me physically ill. The very fact they can be alive while he's suffering as he does is enough to make me want to lose my temper with them."

"Don't do it. Why should they not have to live every day with the consequences of their actions? Both of them are in solitary confinement to keep the other inmates from killing them. To me, being cut off from everything around them is more of a punishment than you ending their time in prison." Tracy looked at them both. "I'm not going to ask you for a promise to kill them. I don't think I have to. What I am going to ask you is, would you not do so? Would you please not kill them while they're in prison?"

"All right." She knew that it had been hard for Mercy to give her what she wanted. Tracy told her she'd owe her for this. "I'll take that too. You will owe me one favor. A favor of whatever I ask, you'll do. I will tell you it will be nothing illegal, nor will it be harmful to you or your brother's health and wellbeing."

They were pulling up in front of the large castle when Tracy put out her hand. Mercy looked at it, then at her. Tracy wasn't sure she would take it at all until she spoke.

"I'm magical, as I'm sure you've gathered. Touching our hands, it will give you something. I'm not sure what, but you will get some of my magic." She smiled at her then. "You'll also get some from all the birds, now that I think on it. This could be really fun."

When she got out of the car, Tracy looked at Joel. He

was grinning as well. She asked him about birds and what that meant. His laughter wasn't very encouraging.

"We're all birds. All of us. I would guess you will be as well." He got out then, and she still sat there.

Mercy looked into the limo where she was still sitting and put out her hand. The moment their fingers touched, Tracy felt it. The tingling down her arm told her she was going to be in deeper shit than she'd realized the moment she and her brother entered the house. But they'd be safe. For her, that was more than enough to put up with a little magic and some tiny birds. What kind of harm could a bird do to her if she messed up? Time would tell, Tracy supposed. Hopefully, she had plenty of time left to figure it out.

Mercy was still laughing as they entered the castle with Abe. Holy crap monkeys, Tracy thought, it really was a castle. And there were beautiful decorations everywhere. Abe just stood in the middle of the great hall and looked around.

"What the hell are you doing here?" The whispered voice could only be one person. "You'll get back into whatever brought you here right this minute and go back to the home. I will deal with you later."

"I sent for them." Tracy turned to look at the beautiful woman standing next to a tall man. "You were told when arrangements were made that everyone was to come to this party. If you want to talk to me about it later, I'll be all ears. But for now, come along, Tracy, my husband and I would like a word with you and your brother Abe."

Tracy followed the woman and her husband to the room with the Christmas tree. While Tracy didn't know exactly what was in store for her at the end of the day, she decided she and Abe would have the best time of their lives today. Tomorrow might find them both locked away again, but the here and now was going to be for them.

Chapter 5

Duncan kept an eye on Mr. Bloom. As soon as he arrived, he became grandda to each and every child he came in contact with. With the adults, he was a little less friendly, but especially Mrs. Holloway. The first words out of the older man's mouth were a snide remark about her so-called job.

When one of the younger kids asked to pull on Mr. Bloom's beard, Duncan was making his way to them when the elderly man laughed and allowed her to pull on it. Duncan was still standing close to him when he reached up to close his mouth.

"You're confused." Duncan nodded. "I wanted to talk to you about something. Something that your new missus spoke to me about when she came out to the house. She sure is a pushy little thing, isn't she?"

"She doesn't have to be pushy with me. I do what she wants." Mr. Bloom said he was a good man for that.

"Why are you here? Not that I mind you coming to see the children. They have so extraordinarily little in their lives as it is. They've taken a shine to you, that's for sure."

"I love children. Always have." The two of them watched as the children played with some of the toys they'd unearthed. "My missus and I weren't blessed with any children. We both wanted them, but I had me something terrible when I was overseas—mumps, of all things. Anyway, when she passed a few years ago, I found myself all alone and not feeling very sociable anymore. You know, you could do a lot for this town if you wanted."

"Such as? I've been working on a few projects. My wife and I are going to help with a couple of things for the schools, as well as the elderly home. What else do you think I should get my hands dirty with?" He nodded toward Ms. Holloway. "I don't think the two of you have been friends. Something I should know about?"

"Yes. Plenty. But I'm only going to tell you what I experienced with her. She don't let them kids go." Duncan didn't understand what he meant. Mr. Bloom walked toward his office, and Duncan followed him inside. Shutting the door seemed to have been all the signal he needed to speak freely. "She's a rotten bitch if you ask me. Me and my missus, as I said, we weren't able to have any children. At the time, she had about a dozen babies there—war babies, they were called back then. Mothers couldn't raise them on their own when the daddy was killed. You understand that story. Anyway, she told us point blank that the kids were for her. She was going to see that they got them a good home. Let me ask you something, young man. Do I strike you as a person that would harm a little fellow? No. I'm telling you right now, I would have given just about anything for us to be able to take one of them babies on. But she kept them, right up until they weren't cute no more. I'm thinking she does something with them. Ain't a soul I know that has gotten a single child out of that place."

"I can look into that—I will look into that. Just give me a second and—" Mr. Bloom asked him what he was. "You mean other than a man? I have a great deal of magic. But for what I might be called, I guess you could say bird. My wife, she's an eagle. Her sisters, all of them, they're birds as well."

"They ain't sisters though, are they? Not that it matters, but a man can see they're closer than any sisters would be. Love you men, too." Duncan said he hoped so. "Plain as the nose on your face that she loves you. You do something with your magic and look into the bitch from the school's head. I know you can do it. Can't you?"

"I can." Duncan could do it, but since he wasn't sure what he would be looking for, he just reached out to her mind. "Christ."

Sitting down, he felt Mr. Bloom fan him with a file he'd had on his desk. It was horrible, the things he'd touched on in her head. Looking at the man he was beginning to like a great deal, Duncan asked him if he really didn't know what she did with the children.

"I'm thinking she is selling them off. That's what I keep telling myself, Duncan. That's what keeps me from being able to sleep at night. If I'm wrong, and I just know I'm not, you need to be telling me." Duncan nodded. "It's something no man would want to know, isn't it?"

"Yes." Duncan stood up and picked up the phone on his desk. "I can take care of it right now. I'm calling in some special help with this. Do you — would you like to be in on this, Mr. Bloom?"

"It's Max, and I surely would."

When the man at the other end answered his phone, Duncan had forgotten about it being Christmas Day. Agent Bishop answered the phone with a laugh and a merry holiday.

"I'm so sorry, Ben. I truly am. But I have a nasty situation here that I need you to move in on now." Ben asked him what had happened, all business as soon as Duncan started out telling him he was sorry. "There is a home in the town where I live for homeless and orphaned children. I have it on good authority the woman and man who are running things there are running a child prostitution ring."

Duncan looked at Max when he sat down, his face as pale as he'd ever seen. Handing the man a bottle of his best bourbon, he wasn't surprised at all when he took the cap off and drank right from the bottle.

Ben knew what Duncan was, that he could see bits and pieces of the future. Also that he could read minds when he needed to. Without Ben questioning his source or the person he might have gotten the information from, Duncan explained to him, in detail, what he'd found in the woman's head.

"When you get in the home, you'll take a left into what looks like a parlor. Behind the bookshelf, you'll find a small room where the pictures and movies are made." Telling him where he would find other incriminating things, Duncan told him that Mr. Bloom, his neighbor, had warned him about her just today. "I would consider it a personal favor to me if you could let him be there when you arrest her."

"What time is your party over today?" Duncan told him they were going to have dinner at five then send them home on the bus. "Good. That's perfect. I'll hit the home now within the hour. Since it's only a little after noon now, I can find enough to go there and have her taken away. The problem is, what happens to the children in the meantime? We have to have a safe place for them to go."

"I can take care of that. I have enough people here and in my area that would gladly help out with this." Duncan looked at Max, who was nodding too. "The kids will be safe, Ben. I promise you this."

After giving him a few more details, the two of them hung up, Duncan looked at Max and asked him if he was all right. When he nodded, then shook his head, Duncan could see that the reality of the situation was much more than even he'd thought. Max asked him what she did with the older children, once they were too old to let her take their pictures.

"She kills them. Max, we wouldn't have been able to stop her without your help. I know it's a lot for you to think about now, but there is no telling how much longer she might well have done this to children." Max nodded but didn't look in his direction. "I can't thank you enough for this. For your help. I'm indebted to you for this."

Still not looking in his direction, Max spoke. "You taking any of those kids for your own?" He told him about the two they were adopting. "There is something I'd like for you to do for me. You don't have to if you don't want to, but I'd appreciate it if you'd allow me to be their grandda. I'd like to have them around me some. Not because I helped out, but just because you want to allow them to come see me."

"They would love it. Perhaps you can talk to Abe some more. I notice he has taken a shine to you." Max nodded. "You can call up anytime you wish to have them come over. I have to make a few phone calls about the children. Do you want to stay?"

"No. I'm feeling the need to get me some more hugs from those kids. You take care that that she-devil don't hurt you none either. I'm just now getting to like you a bit." Max nodded at him, then walked to the door. "You're a good man, Duncan. A damned sight better than I gave you any credit for. I'm sorry for that."

"We're friends now. And to me, I think I've come out on the better end of it."

Max left him there, and Duncan reached out to the woman who had raised him. Mary would be able to find enough homes for all the children in no time flat. He wouldn't be surprised if a few of them found themselves some forever homes after this. Laughing a little, he told Mary what was going on and how many homes he might need.

Is it the little ones at your house now? He told her it was. *I'll make a couple of calls. How about you move it so we can have ourselves an adoption party today too? Might go a long way in getting these kids in a safe home. But tell me, Duncan, what's going on?* He told her everything he'd found out, and even what was going to happen today. *We'll be there. You say about ten families? We'll be there.*

His phone was ringing when he was ready to leave his office. It was Ben, telling him not only had he found the room he'd told him to look for, but there was a lot of paperwork there as well.

"We have everything, Duncan. This is— I'm telling you right now, son, this goes beyond her just running some porn out of this place. We've found a few photo books with newspaper articles, talking about the death of a few of the children she's had in here. Got herself some pictures of before and after they were murdered. This is one sick person. Sicker than I've come across in all my years. She's been doing this for some time too." Duncan told him he was sorry. "I am too. But we're only scratching the surface of things here. We're going to be out to get her. You can count on that. I'm telling you right now, I'm hoping she tries something. I'd be as happy as I've ever been to pop one in the back of her head."

"Tell me when you're going to be here, and I'll make arrangements so the children aren't privy to her being taken out." Ben told him that might be a good idea. "I have people coming for the children soon. Mary told me we might have a huge adoption party going on here today."

"Mary is a good woman. A heart of gold. You tell her for me, she needs anything in taking these children in, I'm there for her. If anyone of them folks she brings to your home needs a reference, I'll stand up and give them my oath that if Mary picks them, they're good people."

Ben told him he'd be there at two. That gave Mary an hour to get there and for the kids to find something to do in the back end of the castle. It might be the perfect time, Duncan thought, to have some cake and ice cream.

By the time he explained to the birds and their mates what was going down, he could tell that not only was Mercy pissed off about it, but Judith looked like she wanted to hunt the woman down right now and end her life. Duncan didn't dare tell her everything Ben had told him. Ms. Holloway would never make it to her next breath if he did that.

Ben had unearthed a mass grave in the back of the home. He'd been able to find it thanks to him being a wolf. The others with him, the officers, had been sickened by the find and had wanted to come along with him when he arrested Hanna Holloway.

At a quarter till two, Mary showed up with not just other people, but gifts they'd brought with them as well. Six families were with the children when Judith herded them to the big dining room for make your own sundaes. Duncan had never been so nervous in his life as he was at this moment.

"What do you think you're doing?" Duncan asked Ms. Holloway what she meant. "I told you when I agreed to this hair-brained idea of yours that they weren't to have too many gifts and that they were not to open them until I approved it. You've got them running like wild animals around here, and I won't have it. I've a good mind to just pack them all up and take them back with me."

"You go ahead and try it. I'm sure that my family will keep you from touching a one of those children. Not to mention, I don't understand why the gifts couldn't be opened. Perhaps you can explain to me why I had to let them open the gifts, then take them away until they were ready to leave." Someone tugged on his shirt, and he turned to find Abe there. "Hello, son. Are you missing the ice−?"

"Do not give that brat any ice cream." Abe grabbed his arm and hid behind him. "Don't you dare try and pit this man against me, Abe. You're not supposed to be here anyway. You're just lucky that we're here, or I'd show you what it means when you try and outsmart me. I'd show you in a moment what it means to you when I give you an order."

Turning his back to the woman, he knelt down in front of Abe. He wasn't a tall child, Duncan realized then. Hugging him to him, Duncan whispered in his ear to go and find his wife and tell her to come to him. After Abe left, it was all Duncan could do to hold onto his temper.

"You ever speak to him like that again, and there will be no finding your body. I'm not making a threat to you, but a promise. There is absolutely no reason whatsoever why he can't be here as well." He heard Judith coming toward them. She was still talking to Abe, he supposed, telling him she was glad he loved ice cream as much as she did. "I'm going to go and have some ice cream with the children. Despite what you're trying to do to them to spoil their fun, they're having a great time. My wife will deal with you."

Duncan kissed Judith when she came into the hall where he was. He told her, so that Ms. Holloway could hear him, that he'd had enough, and his temper was getting the better of him. When she smiled back at him, Duncan thought he'd not want to be Ms. Holloway right now. Judith was going to eat her for lunch.

~*~

Judith just stared at the woman in front of her. There was something so very evil about her that she was surprised she'd not seen it before now. Crossing her arms over her ample chest didn't improve the woman's looks one bit. In fact, Judith laughed at her.

"You're not going to impress me with your show of anger. I've eaten far worse than you when I was just a bird. Though now that I think on it, you are less than the worms and other disgusting creatures that held their people in slavery as king to their realm." She'd confused her, and Judith was fine with that. "I'm a bird, Hanna. A large bird of prey that will most assuredly take you apart if you even try to touch one of these children again."

"You think so, do you? Well, I'm in charge of the little monsters, and I will be gathering them up right now to take them back." When she tried to move around her, Judith blocked her way. "How about if I call the police and have them come and arrest you? I'm sure you and that fancy man you have would just love having you taken away in cuffs."

Judith handed Hanna her cell phone. "Go ahead. Give them a call. I'm sure they might have a few words for you too. By the way, the police are at the home now. They've found your little video recording room." Hanna stiffened, and her face paled to a deathly white. "The mass grave too. It's being excavated as we speak. Also, and this is what I find the most disturbing about you, you've been selling off the children's gifts you have been getting from the state to help them out. I did wonder why you didn't want the gifts played with. You get more money for them if they're pristine, don't you? Or you would have. I'm happy to tell you the police are on their way here, and hopefully, at least as far as I'm concerned, you'll try and escape so that one or all of them have to kill you. But it could be that I just want you dead."

"You don't know what you're talking about." Jude said nothing but walked to the door when the bell rang. "You're going to regret this. See if you don't. You have no idea what you're stepping into with your lies."

The police, about a dozen or so of them, walked into the main hallway where she and Hanna had been speaking. Jamie Nolan, a friend of Duncan's, was front and center. Jude introduced him to Hanna Holloway.

"Yes, ma'am, she's who we're here for." Reading Hanna her rights didn't take all that long. Hanna only glared at her the entire time. Jamie had to ask her twice if she understood her rights as they'd been read to her. "You have to give me an answer, Ms. Holloway. One way or the other. You either understand them, or you don't. Just tell me."

"Oh, I understand a great many things right now. I understand that I'm going to sue each and every one of you for this. I'm going to own this castle once I'm finished with you and that so-called king that you're married to. I have a lot of big names on my list of clients, and I plan to make full use of them. As soon as I make my first phone call, I'm going to be out and coming for the children again. It will be a sad shame if I have to cut costs any way I can."

"You mean the mayor? He's been arrested too. Or do you mean the county seat judge? Sorry to tell you this, but earlier today, he committed suicide. He left a note telling anyone who read it he was sorry for what he'd done." Jude looked at Jamie as she continued. "Your man Peterson and I have been in contact since you were called to the home for children. He's been remarkably busy on his end as well for me."

"I thank you for that, Mrs. Dante. We'll be taking her off your hands now. Also, we've arrested her driver out front. Put up a fuss when we asked him to let us look in the car they came here in. She was apparently making some deliveries. In the name of the Christmas spirit and all, I guess."

Jude couldn't help it, she laughed. It wasn't really funny, but the way he said it, the deadpan look on his face, just tickled her. When they had Hanna in cuffs, Abe came out from behind her and Jude didn't know what to think, or whether to be worried he'd heard too much. But when he stepped up to Hanna, Jude let him have his say.

"She let them hurt me. All the time." Jude got down on her knees and turned Abe to look at her. She asked him what he meant. "They had sex with me, the men she invited to the home—all the time. I'm glad she is going to be gone. I want her dead."

Jude didn't know what to say to the young boy. Pulling him to her, his little body was stiff, ungiving. Holding him, she felt her eyes fill with tears when his tiny arms came up and wrapped around her. Standing with him still in her arm, she turned to Jamie.

"Get this monster out of my home. Now." Jamie hustled her out, not taking the time to allow Hanna to keep up with his long strides. When she fell down, the man dragged her out of the house. The men leaving with her closed the door quietly after they were all gone. "It's never going to happen to you again, Abe. I promise you this on my life, she will never hurt you or any other children so long as I have breath in my body."

"I believe you." He lifted his head from her shoulder and looked at her. "I want you to be my mommy, Judith. I want to live here with you and Mr. Duncan with my— Tracy isn't really my sister. She was helping me get some food when my parents went away, and I went to the home. I love her like my sister. I'm sorry we lied to you."

"It was a good lie, Abe. I'm so incredibly happy she was there for you. And Duncan and I would be happy if you were to be our son and Tracy our daughter. That would make it real—she'd be your sister for real then." He nodded and laid his head back on her shoulder.

Instead of going to the dining room where all the other kids were, she went to the living room and sat down on the couch with Abe still in her arms. There was just too much going on right now, and she needed a moment. More than a moment, she supposed.

"When I was just a bird, an eagle, I would soar up into the clouds to get away from my thoughts. There is nothing more beautiful than a sky beneath you with lines of trees and other things growing in the soil." Thinking of that now, she continued speaking. Jude didn't care if Abe understood what she was telling him, but she did feel better just with the talking. "Once I was changed into a larger bird, bigger than any other creature in the world, I was able to save people from all sorts of things. Once, when a huge storm came up off the water, I sat down on the ground, and hundreds of people came and hid from the worst of it by getting under me. All of us, the other birds, did the same thing. No one was hurt, and everyone was warm and dry. We had to be careful of people getting sick back then. There weren't the kinds of medications we have now."

Jude talked about her life as a bird of prey. How she and the others had been around longer than most people. She thought about the times they'd found castle keeps in worse shape than barns, the people living there all but dead from starvation and illness. The kings of such realms would have so much food in their larders, most of it rotted. Instead of feeding their people, they'd let it go bad.

"Dante wasn't perfect, but to us, she wasn't far from it.

Her people were very loyal to her. She kept them safe from intruders. There was always plenty of food and meat to go around. Even we — her birds, she called us — had plenty to eat and a place to perch." Jude thought of the man who had wedded her, the person who had made her his queen. "I don't remember him, the old king. I suppose he was there while I was nothing more than a bird looking for my next meal. But I saw the people and remembered how there was barely enough for them to eat, much less us. Duncan is his child. Thankfully, from all that was said about the king, Duncan is nothing like him. I love him. Duncan, I mean. He's the best parts of his mother and a good man."

She knew Abe had fallen asleep. Jude could well imagine the child hadn't had a good night's sleep in a long time. Without the help of Tracy, she was sure the little boy would have perished long ago.

Jude wondered if Tracy had been abused as Abe had. She did think about looking to see. The answer would have been right there in her mind for Jude to look into. However, she decided to wait for the girl to tell her. If it became an issue, then she'd look. But for now, Jude decided it would be all right if Tracy had some secrets she didn't want to share.

Being a mother had never occurred to her. Not even as a bird had it ever crossed her mind to take a mate and have some hatchlings. There might have been a time she would have. But meeting Dante and being her bird was something she was immensely proud of. Raising a hatchling might have been too dangerous back in those times. There was forever someone stealing eggs from birds for food.

"Are you all right?" Jude smiled at Duncan when he spoke quietly. "You'll be happy to know that every child has a parent. They'll be permanent homes for them too, I think."

"I'd like to help each of the families out. Add onto their homes. Build some playground equipment for them all to use. Food, too, if they might need it." Duncan came into the room more and sat on the sofa across from her and Abe. "You know what happened in here, don't you? I can't repeat it. It's like a stone stuck in my throat every time I think about the things she did to these children."

"Yes, Jamie told me while it was going on. I'm so sorry." Jude told him she wasn't hurt by Hanna, but the kids were. "But you had to hear it from her mouth. I've contacted a couple of doctors I know to come and talk to the kids. They might not all need help, but the few that do, I want them to have someone close by. I was going to ask you if you were sure about taking these two, but I think I have my answer."

"You do. I've fallen in love with them both. The way that Tracy protects him. Mercy said she was all up in her face at the home until she found out they were bringing the two of them here." Duncan nodded. "We really should make our marriage a reality, don't you think? I mean, everyone already refers to me as Judith Dante."

"I think that's a wonderful idea." He pulled a small box from his pants pocket. "This was in with the jewelry that Mom left me. I think she had it made rather than it coming from the spoils of war. It meant a great deal to her, and in turn, it means that much to me too. Will you wear it? I mean, will you marry me, Judith Castle? My queen of all that we rule?"

The ruby was about the size of a quarter. Dark with age, it was flawlessly cut and shone in bright colors all around the room. Even the Christmas tree paled in comparison to its beauty and shine.

"I will. Gladly." They kissed, both of them being careful not to wake Abe. But just as they were going to kiss a second time, the children came racing into the room. They had great news, Mary told them. Each child had a new mommy and daddy.

"How wonderful for all of you." Jude looked at the other birds and thanked them for their help while Duncan talked about how they'd be having so much fun living with each of their new families.

Mercy leaned back on the couch when Abe woke to play with the other children. When asked for permission to play with their new toys, each parent got down on the floor and helped them take things out of the packaging. This was what she needed, a perfect end to this day.

She and Duncan played several games with the kids and ate too much sugary food. Then she fell asleep in his arms as soon as the other children were taken to their new homes. Neither of them cared that they were sleeping on the couch, their children asleep on the floor in new sleeping bags.

Chapter 6

Piper was just packing away the last of her things when someone rang her doorbell. She'd not wanted to be interrupted, but duty called. As soon as she flung the door open, she knew something had happened.

"What is it?" Aryne Peterson asked if he could come in. Inviting him in was easy—getting information from him was another matter altogether. "If you don't start talking, I might well have to hurt you. What is it?"

"The Martins. The ones that had their home burnt down just before Christmas." He looked around. "I hadn't realized you'd found a place to live. Shall I congratulate you now?"

"I'm moving back to where I came from. All of us are." Aryne looked so crestfallen that she nearly laughed. "We'll be coming back from time to time. And I'll make sure you have my new number once I'm settled. We decided that we love it back there. It's our roots, I guess you could call it.

My sister Jude, she's marrying the king of the place there. She'll be his queen in all things."

"That's wonderful. I'm so happy for all of you. Not so much about you leaving the area, but that you're going to be all together. But about the Martins. They're claiming I've doctored my report on what I found out there. That I poured gasoline all around so their insurance wouldn't pay off. I'm glad more every day that you bought me the body cam I've been using. The recording of it all, including our conversation out there, is being reviewed by the sitting judge." Piper asked him why he'd come to her. "You're going to be called as a witness. It's not a bad thing. The judge, I believe you know him—Arthur Montgomery. He likes you and said that if he was to trust anyone with the truth, it would be you. He asked me to come by here and let you know he was going to have you summoned."

"When is it?" Aryne smiled. "Today? He is making this thing start today? What would have happened had I not been home? Would he have just waited me out?"

"Yes. As I said, he likes you and knows you're going to be honest with the court. He is going to tell the Martins you were on scene with me." Piper asked him what capacity she was testifying in. "He's making you a part of the fire team, as the one to head up things like this, discordances with insurance companies and families. I think you'd be a pro at it. Not to sound mean, but you don't take shit from anyone, and that would put you in favor of anyone I know. A straight shooter is what he said."

She looked around her apartment. There really wasn't

much left to do. She was just making herself busy work, so she'd not be in the middle of something when she was to meet with her sisters. It was their party night, the only night of the week they were able to get together as a family.

"I can do this, but I won't miss my dinner date with the family. You know as well as I do that we get together every Wednesday night. It's our time." Aryne told her he knew that and had told Montgomery that too. "When do I have to be there?"

For an answer, Aryne went to the door and opened it. Shaking her head, she hated to admit that she wanted to do this. And doing it before she tore the reasons apart as to the reason she wanted to do it would be good for her. She tended to overthink things.

The courtroom was filled, a surprise to her since it was only a couple of days after Christmas. When she asked where she should be seated, Judge Montgomery called for her to come to the seat next to him. As soon as she was seated, he handed her some files. The one on top was from the Martins. The others, she remembered, she'd been to the sites of the fires with Aryne. She looked up when someone said her name.

"What makes you an expert on the fire at the Martin home, Ms. Warrior? I'm to understand that you're some sort of artist. The last time I was in college, that wasn't considered a degree." There was a little bit of laughter around the otherwise quiet room when the attorney for the Martins spoke. Piper smiled. If he'd known her, even a little, he would have backed off then. "What do you have to add to this that the fire marshall called you in today to help with?"

He made quotation marks with his fingers when he said *help*, like he was implying something else besides her helping in any way. Whatever had he meant by it? Well, it pissed her off enough for her to get as nasty as he'd been.

"I have degrees in law enforcement and emergency medical services. I also have a doctorate in fire sciences and forensic fire investigations. I'm a retired firefighter with the 151 here in town too." The men and women present today shouted "hoo-hoo," as they did at this particular firehouse every time they met up with one of their own. The attorney for the Martins, Tyler Peck, said she seemed to be overqualified for the job. "How would you know what I'm qualified or even overqualified to do? You're an attorney, and I can do your job as well if you want to know the truth. So far? I'm not terribly impressed by you at all."

"Be that as it may, what do you have to say about the fires that the Martins have had?" She told him everything she'd figured out about the fire. Since he didn't put any kind of stipulations on which fire, she was able, after the judge said Peck should be more careful how he worded things, to bring up the other fire the Martins had too. "The first fire has nothing to do with this fire, Your Honor. Why is she bringing that up?"

"Because, as you were told, you didn't say which fire. The first fire wasn't a total loss for the Martins. That one also had a very distinct smell of gasoline. If I were to speculate on how the fire was contained to the front of the home,

I'd say it was the fire department who saved most of the home. The insurance company they had, the one they had doubled their insurance policy on within two days before the fire, said they could build onto the remaining house." She pulled out the picture that was in the file of the crime scene of the second fire. "The second fire, as you can see here, took down the entire house. I'd like to say it was a total loss, but I can't. The barn and several places that you can put items in to store were filled with their belongings. The only things left in the house that we could find were two cans of dog food, a couch older than the house, as well as some broken toys. Before you ask me how I knew they were broken, they were in melted pieces when they were retrieved from the fire."

Peck just stared at her. She smiled at him again when she told him that was her professional opinion as an artist too. Piper flipped to the second picture and brought it up so everyone could see. Before she could talk about it, Peck interrupted her again.

"Ms. Warrior, I'm sure you have a great deal of what you might consider evidence to the contrary, but the Martins have lost their home. Everything they hold dear to their hearts. Everything you're saying right now is only your opinion. What if I told you I have a person here in the courtroom today that discounts every part of your testimony?" Piper told him to bring them in. She'd compare her notes with his. "Are you telling me and this courtroom that you're a better expert than the person I have? That's sort of prejudiced, isn't it?"

She stared at him for a moment. "What the hell are you talking about? I in no way implied, nor said, that I was better than anyone. I said—quite nicely, I think—that I'd compare notes with his. I never once, not ever in my career, said I was better than anyone." He stared at her, his face getting redder by the moment. Not from embarrassment, but because his anger at her was filtering through his flippant attitude. "Are you going to call out your witness, or are you going to stand here like a fish with your mouth hanging open?"

Piper glanced down at the paperwork she'd been handed. Pulling out the second set of pictures, she stared it for several seconds before something about the name occurred to her. Reaching out to the others, Piper asked if one of them could look something up for her. It was Duncan who answered her call.

Sure. I'm sitting in front of the computer now. What do you need? She told him what she thought she'd found on the files. *That shouldn't take long. So, you think this is a family affair, do you? Well, well, well. You're correct. Mrs. Patti Hanger is the sister to Mr. Denny Martin. And guess what? As you have figured out, Mr. Martin has a stepbrother who also suffered a tragic fire to his home. Mr. Garland's home was a total loss as well. Let me check on something else for you here.*

When Peck asked her a question, she asked for a moment. Shuffling around the papers, she was getting a better timeline of the things going with the fires. Then Duncan got back to her with more information.

They used different insurance companies for each home.

Garland actually went to one out of state to cover his ass. Also, I was able to pull up some records with rental storage units. Each of them rented two storage units a week before the fires. I'm sure if we were to go and look, we'd see pretty much the same furniture in them that they're claiming to have been destroyed in the fires. What else can I do for you, Piper?

You've done more than I thought I'd have right now. She smiled at Peck when he asked her if she was going to answer his question, a question she had no idea he'd asked. *I have to go. Pecker head is wanting some information from me.*

Duncan was laughing as she closed up the connection. He was still there, of course, but he was no longer speaking to her. When Piper asked Montgomery for a wipe-off board, he said he had one in his office. While it was being brought out, Piper made notes on the timeline of each of the fires and what the families had done leading up to it. This was going to be epic.

She was invited to have lunch with Montgomery after the arrests were made, and everyone was finished laughing. It had been funny, and having all her ducks in a row like she had really put Peck on the defense. He also was fined for contempt of court when he wouldn't shut up while she was explaining her information.

Declining the invite was overrun when Montgomery took her by the hand and nearly dragged her to the little café inside the courthouse. She'd not even been aware there was one here. Enjoying a nice thick roast beef sandwich, Montgomery told her what his plan was for her.

"I'm not sure you heard, but I'm moving. Soon." He

told her it didn't matter where she lived, so long as she was able to go to suspicious fire scenes. "You're meaning all of them, aren't you?"

"I am. You'll be well compensated. Insurance will be paid by the state you're working in. Also, all hotel and accommodations you need to stick around for a couple of days will be paid directly to you. For all court appearances you need to be in on, like today, you'll be given a bonus if you win—which I have to admit, you really did a bang-up job on this one." She thanked him and thought about the deal he was offering her. She asked about her art. "Yes, I did explain to the governor that you were a renowned artist, and that would take you out of commission for some time. It was explained to me that the scene would be held until such time as you could go and look it over. You're getting just about anything you want or need in this, Piper. I've never seen them bending so far over for someone before."

"You said I was getting just about anything. What is it you think I should ask for too?" He laughed. "I've known you a long time, Montgomery. Spill it."

"Piper, you've made me what I am today. I hope you know that. Without you picking me up out of the gutter and giving me a good knocking around, I'd be dead. Or wish I was." She told him it wasn't that much. "It was to me and my family. I will never, for as long as I live, forget what you did for me and my family. Ever. In answer to your question, the only thing I can see you might want to ask for is that you don't give them an answer right away. Perhaps they'll sweeten the pot for you. So to speak."

"You sly old devil you. You already told them I was going to be a hard sell, didn't you? Just to make them think on ways to improve my package." He told her she'd taught him that. "So I did. I'll need time to think, as you suggest—about a week. I should be in my home by then and things going in the correct direction for me. I need this move. I need to be with my family."

"I understand that. The six of you, you've been together longer than most housing developments have been. I'm incredibly happy for you and your family." She nodded and told him she had to get going. "All right. I'll tell them you need the week. If you need more, which I'd not push if I were you, then that'll be all right as well."

Piper felt good as she was making her way back to her apartment. She felt so wonderful, in fact, that she decided to go and see about finding some furniture for her home. According to Duncan, it would be finished in a few days, as well as her studio. Going into the large warehouse they stored their things in when they redecorated, Piper knew just what she was looking for. It was time to have some of her own kind of fun.

~*~

Jude waited in the waiting room for Tracy to be examined by a doctor. She had to have a physical to enter the local school district. Abe was with Duncan seeing another doctor. Tracy was as nervous as Jude was about coming here. Doctors hadn't played a large part in her life until now. Nervous over what? No clue, Jude thought. Just something she was feeling about her children a great deal lately.

Abe and I are finished. I'm glad you were able to find him a doctor that specialized in trauma patients. He examined him and said he was fit but small for his age. Also, he asked Abe if he wanted to talk to him alone about anything. The kid surprised me and told the doctor that for now, he had a new family, and we were helping him. She felt her heart swell up with the thought of being able to help this child. *He's really smart too. Tomorrow when we take them to be tested for their grade to be put in, I'm going to crow like a rooster when they tell me he's brilliant.*

I hope you're not disappointed. Duncan told her he could never be disappointed in their children. *I'm awfully glad to hear that. By the way, I need to take Tracy shopping. They don't have too much in the way of clothing. But I did tell her we'd find a place that wasn't Walmart. It's not that it's a bad place to shop, but I want her to have something that is her style. Not something that was on sale and all she could have.*

Abe is the same way. I told him he was going to need a heavier coat and some boots. He was thrilled to know he could have them both at the same time, and they'd be new. I hate that these kids, all of them, were treated like they were. I'm not discounting the things that Hanna did to them in this, but they should have had a great deal more than she was providing for them. Jude agreed with him. *All right. We're going to the mall. Maybe we can meet up later and have dinner together. I know it's New Year's Eve, but I can't think of a better group to be bringing the new year in with than my new family.*

When Tracy came out to the waiting room with her, Jude didn't ask her what was said. Instead, she went up to pay for the visit and to set up a second one in six months. As they were going down to the main floor in the elevator, Tracy started laughing. She asked her what was so funny.

"You're about to bust, aren't you? In wanting to know what sort of shape I'm in." Jude felt her face heat up in embarrassment. "You can ask me, Jude. I won't get all pissy with you. I'm fine, he told me. Undernourished a bit. I told him where we were coming from, and he said he was glad I've become a family member of yours. He told me you helped him get through med school."

"I provided him the money to go to college. What he did with it was whatever he wanted. What kind of food did he recommend for you to eat? By the way, Abe is fine as well. Undernourished, the same as you. We plan on making sure you have anything you want to eat—I guess within reason. You don't want to get too over nourished, do you? You can if you want. Whatever makes you happy." Tracy told her she made her happy. "Thank you. I'm so glad to hear that today. It's been a rough morning for me."

"Anything I can help you with?" Jude thought about it and decided if she really wanted to help, she'd let her. "I'm game for just about anything. I sort of owe you for saving us."

"You don't really think that, do you?" Tracy turned to look at her as they were in the parking garage. "I mean, we didn't take you in because we wanted you to owe us something. You don't believe we did it for any other reason than we wanted you two to become our family, do you?"

"Honestly?" Jude nodded, getting herself ready for

some sort of horrible thoughts coming from Tracy as to why they'd adopted them. "When you and Duncan first told us what you were doing, I was ready to take Abe and head out. I don't have any idea where we might have ended up—probably on the wrong end of something bad. But I saw you holding Abe. He was asleep in your arms as if he belonged there."

"Just me holding him? That got you to stay?" Tracy told her it was because he'd been asleep. "I'm sorry. I'm not trying to be dense here, but why did that make you want to stick around with us? I'm assuming you trusted us for that reason."

"No. It was because Abe trusted you. Enough so that he was able to fall asleep without me there to keep him safe. He trusted that you'd not hurt him. Not make him feel like he had to have someone protecting him while he was resting. He trusted you. And in turn, I did as well." Jude looked at Tracy. "Do you understand now?"

"Yes. I do. And I want to thank you for telling me. I don't know what I'd do if I were to find either of you gone from the house. I would move heaven and earth to keep you both safe." Jude thought about what she was saying. "I know you and Abe have only been with us for about a week now, but I feel as if you've opened up a part of my heart that I hadn't realized was closed off. Duncan moved in there too but in a different sort of way. I've fallen in love with both of you. You mean more than anything to me."

Tracy hugged her. Not just a quick hug where her arms barely touched her before she moved away, but a full out, entire body hug that warmed her all the way to her heart. Hugging her back, telling her how much she loved her, she was a little sad when Tracy pulled back and looked up at her. The tears in her eyes brought Jude's to the point of falling down her cheeks.

"Thank you, Mom." Jude burst into tears when Tracy called her mom. It was more than she had hoped for when taking these kids to her heart. "We should get going. I don't know about you, but all this emotional crap is making me hungry."

It took her a couple of minutes to gather herself enough to drive. While she was sitting there in the car, she had a sudden thought. Looking at Tracy, she wondered why she'd not said anything about driving. Asking her why she didn't drive had the girl laughing again.

"Because there wasn't a car around for me to practice in mostly. Not to mention, it's doubtful that Hanna would have allowed me to drive her car." Jude asked her if she'd had the permit test. "No. It didn't occur to me until just now that I could be driving. I have driven before—not legally, but I have driven. Are you going to buy me a car if I say I'd like to drive?"

Sure she was joking, Jude told her she would buy her a good stable car. "I don't want you out someplace where you can't get home. You and Abe, you both need cell phones as well. I know we told you about how we can communicate with you since we've taken you into our hearts, but you need to have a phone for other things too." Jude pulled out of the doctor's parking lot and onto the road. "I've never been big on driving. I guess you could say my way of getting around pleases me where driving doesn't. I don't like traffic. People, for the most part, are all right, but I don't like them in traffic."

"I think it's a given that if there is traffic, you can bet there will be people in the cars." Jude grinned at her. She had such a good sense of humor. "But I don't expect you to give me whatever I want. That's not the way it's supposed to work."

"It's how I work. I won't give either of you everything, but I will indulge you in some things. Having a reliable car isn't an indulgence, however. It's a necessity. For both of us—my peace of mind, and your ability to go from point A to B without getting into a terrible accident." Tracy said she could understand her wanting her to be safe. "Good. Because I didn't mention this to you before, but you're an immortal. You'll age until you're about twenty-five, then you'll just stay the way you are. You won't be able to gain weight after that, either. Just to let you know."

"Duncan told me this morning before I left home. He also mentioned that I'm a princess. I thought he was just calling me a nickname, but I've been thinking about it, and he literally called me a princess. Princess Tracy of the Dante Castle. How flipped out is that?" Tracy laughed a little. "I think Abe took his being a prince to his head. He was making me call him that before they left for Abe's appointment."

"If you think that is flipped out, try having people call you queen." They were both laughing when they pulled up in front of the boutique she'd been telling Tracy about. "I know the people who have this shop. They're both a part of the families Dante moved to New Town before it was destroyed. They're both fae, so I want you to be prepared for anything. There are only dresses and other things in their shop for any humans that come around. You're no longer human, so you'll be able to see what they want you to see."

"What do you mean, I'm no longer human? Not to mention, there are faeries around too?" Jude got out of the car and made her way to the front of the store while Tracy hammered her with questions. "Mom? Are they going to turn me into something?"

"Not unless you piss them off." Opening the door, Jude inhaled deeply. It was different for every person that came inside this particular shop. The scent was meant to calm a person. A stressed person couldn't shop well, she'd been told. "What do you smell, Tracy?"

"Almonds. Toasted and buttery. Also, I smell fresh vanilla. Why can I smell this?" Jude told her that was her calming tool. That the smells she had were associated with a good calm memory for her. "My grandma. She made toasted almonds to put over vanilla ice cream as a treat for me. I miss her."

Jude hated to shop and had always used the magic she had to dress herself whenever she needed to go someplace. But hanging out with Tracy, having her try different things on, was the most fun she'd had in an exceptionally long time. As she stood in front of the mirror with a pair of dress slacks and a large sweater that was, surprisingly enough, a bright pink in color, Tracy looked at her in the reflection.

"I would never have liked this outfit if you hadn't made me try it on. I love the color so much now that all I want are pink tops." Jude said it looked great on her too. "I love this. The jeans too. Can I get the pink tennis shoes to go with this? I know it's winter, but this is so beautiful."

"You can't wear tennis shoes in the snow, no. But you have to have something on your feet when you're in school. And if you don't get the pink shoes that go well with that, then I'm going to be upset. It really looks amazing." Tracy squealed in delight. The rush to get the shoes had her laughing too. "You might want to pick up a few colors of shoes, Tracy. Pink doesn't go with everything."

The man in the shop with them wasn't anyone she knew. Making sure there was nothing between him and her, Jude kept an eye on him. But when Daisy came out of the backroom and hugged him tightly, Jude did let down her guard. She had to shake the tenseness off—she'd been so ready to kill him if he'd tried anything stupid.

"Jude, I'd like for you to meet my son. This is Grant. He has adopted, as we all have, the last name of Coby. Grant, this is the new queen. Duncan and Jude are getting married as soon as the weather warms up again." She shook his hand when it was offered, and felt the blast of power up her arm. He wasn't just fae, she realized.

"I'm a little of everything, my lady. When I was born, there was a terrible storm brewing. Once I took my first breath, it was obvious I wasn't going to make it." Jude said he felt to her like he was brownie and faerie too. "That's right. Also, a little wolf added in, just in case. I was able to survive simply because I was given all their magic. My mother said it's also what makes me a stubborn ass."

They were both laughing when Tracy joined them. After introducing her to the man, Tracy went to try on another set of clothing. Grant and his mother headed to the backroom to talk. It was then that Piper contacted her to tell her what was going on.

You're bringing Tracy to dinner tonight, aren't you? She'd forgotten about it but knew that Duncan would understand. *That kid, she's going to fit right in with us. I've been talking to her about the things she might want to study at college. I think it only hit her then that she was going to be able to go. You've done a great thing for them, Jude. We all think so.*

They've done a great thing for me too. She told her how she'd called her mom for the first time. *Right now, we're getting her some clothing. When I mentioned to her she could just change her outfits, she hadn't any idea what she would like. This is helping her be able to make choices. We're going to purchase some of them too. I can't imagine the things they put up with at that home.*

I've been doing some research for Duncan about the place. Some of the shit those kids had to endure is beyond what any person in a jail cell would have had happen to them. I'm so awfully glad, the more I find out that the kids are no longer there. Oh, Mary called me today. She said to tell you that all the children are adapting well and are having a good time. Some of them have been terrified they might be sent back if they misbehave. That's what they're working with now, I guess. Making sure they understand they're in their forever homes. Jude gave Tracy a thumbs up when she came out in a cute skirt with another baggy sweater. *I'll see you tonight. I can almost taste your enjoyment you're having there.*

After telling Duncan she had plans for this evening, he sounded happy. Apparently, he and Abe were going to see who could eat the most pizza. The other men were joining them as well. Jude was happy, very much so. She couldn't wait for the next bird to find a mate. Jude didn't care who it was either.

Chapter 7

Hanna didn't know what all the fuss was about. Sure, she'd done some terrible things in the name of taking care of children. But what the hell did they think she was going to live in with the stipend they paid her monthly? It was barely enough for her to buy food each month. There was never enough money left over each payday for her to have a social life. Not that she had one of those anymore either.

Hanna hated people, but not the money they provided her with. That was golden. And as far as she could understand from these idiots that had arrested her, they'd not been able to open her safe and couldn't find the other money. Porn, it seemed, was a huge moneymaker. Baby porn was even more profitable.

Two people sat in the chairs behind hers. She didn't pay all that much attention to faces. Hanna had always been a clothing snob. Not that she wore the latest fashions or the most hip wear. She tended to wear things she'd purchased until they were little more than strings and rags. Even then, she'd turn them into something serviceable. She didn't get to be wealthy by being stupid with her funds.

She'd known someday she'd be caught. What had surprised Hanna now was that it had taken them this long to figure it out. That was another reason she hated people. They were stupid as donkeys. Turning back in her seat to face the front when no one else came in, she tried to figure out what to say to these people to make her have a lighter sentence. Nothing much came to mind. Hanna knew she was going to serve some jail time.

It might be nice, she thought, to not have to listen to whiney brats all day. Not have to figure out if someone buying her product was really a nasty person or the cops. Either way, she was due for a little rest and relaxation time. Mostly, she thought, she'd be able to not have to put up with her brothers. Harland and George were the only family she had left. They also depended on her for every little thing they needed.

Harland was mentally challenged. That was the fancy term they'd put on him when he'd failed preschool all those years ago. Since their parents died, she'd been responsible for him. It was tough going at times, but he had his usefulness too. Like when he had to dig a hole. He'd dig to China if she didn't go out and tell him to stop, it was deep enough.

George was plain stupid. He never got jokes. Even if you took the time to explain them to him, he would still stare at you as if you had three heads, for Christ's sake. He didn't care for fun. And worst of all, he hated to be dirty. He showered several times a day without fail. Also, his hands were raw because he would use hand sanitizer until it literally ate away at his skin.

When the bailiff came to tell everyone to stand, she didn't on principle. No one stood up when she entered the room, and to her, it was a waste of time to get up and down like she was some sort of jack in the box.

The judge — Harmon, if she read the placard correctly — cocked a brow at her. She didn't pay him any mind. This was going to be an all-day event anyway. Being as old as she was, getting up and down like he thought he deserved was hard on her old bones. Once again, she thought some jail time would be perfect right about now.

As soon as the doors were closed behind her, she didn't bother waiting on someone to ask her to speak. Standing up, because she wanted to have his full attention, she cleared her throat when he asked her what she had to say.

"Plenty, as a matter of fact. But for now, I want to plead guilty." He asked her if she knew what the charges were. "I haven't any idea what sort of crap was concocted on my behalf. But I want to plead guilty to it. All of it, as a matter of fact."

"I see. Do you have an attorney? It says here that you've refused the one assigned to you." She didn't point out how he'd asked a question he already had the answer to but told him she didn't need one. "I see. So, I'm to assume you don't care what the charges are against you. You're just going to assume it's nothing to get you into too much trouble and be done with it. I'm sorry to say, it's not going to work like that with this trial. There are a great many people who are going to need to hear what you were doing out there under the guise of caring for children."

"I'm assuming you mean the porn videos?" He didn't even blink at her. "Yes, yes. I did those. I wasn't getting enough money by being a nice person. That was what I had to do to care for those brats and my family. I did it. Move on."

"Be that as it may, I'm going to tell you now, there will be a trial, as well as witnesses and the entire gamut of things that happen in a courtroom. It's what I get paid to do." He hit his gavel on the desk like that was supposed to be taken as fact. "Is there anything else, Ms. Holloway? As it stands right now, you're already getting on my nerves. It's only eight-thirty in the morning too."

"I'm well aware of what the time is. Even though they took my watch from me, I know the time without a clock better than most. I'm not going to sit through a trial with you. I told you, I'm guilty. I just want to get on with the sentencing and be done with you. This is a total waste of my tax dollars." She gave him her best "I'm not fucking around with you" stare, but he only laughed. "And what, pray, do you find so funny?"

"You. Especially if you think this display of temper or whatever it is you're trying to convey to me by your look is going to get you anywhere. I'm married to a beautiful Irish woman who has the temper to match her fine red hair and freckles. If you think to even get close to what I've put up with over the last thirty some years, then you're sadly mistaken." He laughed a little more before continuing. "Now, have a seat, Ms. Holloway, before I have you removed to be shackled. I've suddenly decided that having you here for this entire trial might be the most fun I've had in some time. *Sit down.*"

She was sitting before she could think about it. He had used the mojo stuff on her, which meant he wasn't a good Christian human, such as she was. What was this world coming to when every Tom, Dick, and Harry could simply take over the jobs of humans that needed it?

They droned on about all the things she'd done. It wasn't as if anyone in this room didn't know she'd been caught. Most of these idiots thought she was wrong for doing something to provide for her family. People needed to get their heads out of their asses and think about the things she'd had to give up while she'd been doing the job of keeping kids off the street.

You don't honestly think you did the right thing in this, do you? She looked around for who was speaking to her. *I'm in the room with you, Hanna, but I'm not close enough to speak to you directly. I do believe that sitting next to you would be dangerous — for you, not me. I'd strangle you where you sit and not have a single thought about it.*

"Who is this?" Everyone stopped talking to look at her. "There is someone here speaking to me, and I want to know who it is."

No one can hear me, but you. You're only making a fool of yourself — or I should say, a bigger fool of yourself — by talking about me. She asked the person again who dared to speak to her. *Dares? I suppose you would find it as a cut on your personality to have someone like me speaking to you. You don't like shifters, do you?*

"They're an abomination to the world. Where are you? I want to know who this is." He told her not to speak aloud, or she'd never find out what they had to say. "I'll do as I want, you bastard. Where are you?"

As I said, here in the room with you. Go ahead and speak to me aloud. They'll only think you're insane and lock you up in an institution someplace. I, however, don't think you'd enjoy that overly much. The people there, the criminally insane, would have it in their heads that you're a monster. More so than they might be. People, shifters or not, they don't take kindly to having children killed. Especially ones so young as a month. She thought of all the things she could say to him on that score. *Ah, so you've thought about it, have you? Well, think of this. When they put you into a room with equal criminals such as yourself, they'll latch onto you like you're fresh meat — a new face. You won't be able to get away from them. Then one night, when you're trying your best to ignore them, the staff will turn their back on the room, and you'll end up dead. Did I tell you how much people hate your sort of murderer?*

Hanna had to think about how to answer without speaking when it occurred to her to just think her answers. *I don't care what they call me. I will not be put into an insane place either. I'm not crazy.* He asked her why she thought she wasn't. *I'm as sane as anyone. I needed more money than they were paying me.*

I don't think they could have paid you nearly enough for you to have stopped what you were doing. You seemed to enjoy it too much, I'd say. She didn't have to answer—she had enjoyed some aspects of the movie-making. *Why was it necessary for you to kill them off when you were finished with them? Why not allow them to be adopted instead of killing them, then burying them in the back yard as you did?*

Children have no concept of keeping their mouths shut. If they'd mentioned me at all and what we were doing, then I would have been caught decades ago. He told her it sounded as if she had enjoyed that as well. *Killing them? I suppose I did in some way. They were forever wanting this or that. What did they expect me to do, shit a toy out for them? As it was then, I'd have to take all the gifts they were given and sell them off. Do you have any idea how much it costs daily to feed them? More than you make in a month, I'm betting.*

I'm sure you thought so. But it's doubtful you were spending all that much. I have heard what you were feeding them. Oats two meals out of three? Then peanut butter sandwiches the other meal? No meat except on Sundays? Hanna told him she was working on a budget. *You mean a budget for the children. Just the night before you were arrested, you and your brothers had steaks along with large baked potatoes. That wasn't just one of either. You and the other two ate like that every night of the week. What a shame you won't get those sorts of meals while in prison.*

She didn't bother pointing out to him that she'd had to keep house daily. Make sure the kids had a bath, food, and some sort of learning craft. It took a lot out of her to do such things. Not to mention, fending off all the people who wanted to take her from her job. Keeping a home full of children from potential deadbeat parents was a full-time job.

Oh, and don't forget the time it took you to make and sell your side job. I don't know how you were able to live with yourself doing what you did. Again, there wasn't any reason for her to answer him. He'd just make some sort of snide remark back to her. *I'd never do that. I'm a nice person. It's you that is the monster in all this.*

This time she turned to find him. There was no doubt in her mind that she'd be able to pick him out. The man was going to pay for talking to her this way. When his laughter echoed through her mind, she glared harder at each man until they looked in her direction.

You won't figure it out, I'm afraid. You're assuming I'm a man when I'm not. I'm not human either. I can change myself into whatever creature and person I want to be. How about I give you a little hint? The laughter again. *Look to your right, Hanna, and I'll prove to you what I mean.*

Looking to her right, she saw nothing. Then as she was looking again, just to be sure, she saw herself sitting in a chair at the back of the room. The little wave had her waving back. Hanna turned in her chair so quickly it tipped in a way she was sure she was going to hit the floor. However, with the tilting of it and her weight, the chair broke and splintered under her.

Getting herself upright proved to be more difficult than she thought it should have been. It wasn't until she was standing up, holding onto the table for a moment, that she realized she'd been hurt. The blood running down her leg worried her. It was a steady stream that had her sick to her belly.

"Are you all right?" She glared at the man who was helping her. "I'm only asking because a woman your age cannot afford to break a hip."

If she hadn't had to hold onto the table to stand up, she would have slapped the piss right out of him—the nerve of some people. Glaring at him didn't seem to work either, as he wasn't looking at her face. Finally, she felt something hard hit the back of her legs, and she plopped down. It was undignified, but she was sitting rather than holding onto a wobbling table.

"I've called an ambulance." She told the judge it wasn't necessary, she was fine. "Perhaps you should look at the piece of wood that has become a part of your body, Ms. Holloway. You're bleeding badly too."

Looking down, she saw the sliver of wood that was indeed in her calf. It was making her ill again, so she looked away. The blood pooling under the table and chair was bad enough, but the wood sticking out both sides of her leg like an arrow was too much. Getting dizzy now, she felt sick and thought she might pass out as well. Damn it all to hell, she thought. This was going to drag things out longer than she wanted.

~*~

Jude watched the proceedings. The ambulance drivers were trying their best not to puke on their patient, while the others in the room were using their phones to send what had happened out to the masses. She wondered briefly how they'd gotten their phones in here. She'd been asked to leave hers in the car.

Not that she didn't feel bad for Hanna being hurt. She had been teasing her, and that had made her angry. That was what she wanted, not her being hurt to the point she had to be taken away in an ambulance. Getting up, careful of the men working, Jude slipped out of the courtroom and into the bright sunlight.

You seem pissy right now. She told Mercy she wasn't so much pissy as disappointed. *Having her in jail and awaiting trial couldn't have happened to a more terrible person if you ask me. They're still pulling blankets from the ground over here. So far, they've unearthed three dozen blanket wrapped bodies. That's fucking sick.*

Are you just standing there watching them? She told her she was in a tree looking down on them. *I'm sure that's not scary or anything. I'd be scared if I looked up into a naked tree and saw a large falcon sitting there staring down at me.*

No one has noticed me. I think they're set on this job. Did you hear that her brother George has been hospitalized? She told her that she hadn't. *I guess he's some kind of germophobe. When one of the officers touched him to cuff him, he went berserk. After they took him to the jail, giving him his bottle of hand sanitizer back to him, he drank it. He was heard saying it was the only way to get all the germs off him. He's also being treated for his hands. I guess they're a mess as well.*

This is one fucked up family. Hanna is on her way to the hospital as well. Jude told her what had happened. *It was sort of my fault. I was having fun with her when she was startled while turning in her chair. I'm not really sorry about it. Hanna deserves what she gets. However, I think this might be a good thing. They might have all the bodies accounted for by the time she's ready to come back. Didn't she have two brothers? Harland, I think that was the other one's name.*

That's right. He's not competent to stand trial. The officer that arrested him while he was in the yard got socked in the face when George started screaming. The officer wouldn't allow Harland to go to his brother, and that caused a ruckus. When the doctor at the hospital was treating his wounds — the other officers took him to the ground, and he was cut — and started talking to him about what had happened, the doc said he could barely comprehend anything that was going on around him. Even his last name was something he wasn't able to think of. Jude asked her if Hanna had been talked to, to see if she had any mental instabilities. *Not that I'm aware of. But then, she was in a jail cell when the other two were arrested. I would guess they should test her, don't you think?*

I think it's a given that she's nuts. Mercy laughed. *The thing is, I've been through her mind. She's all right with being arrested. In fact, she's thinking of it as a kind of vacation.*

Along with the trip in her mind, I have found out where her money is. And she's amassed a fortune, too. I have an idea it should be used for the burial of these children. Barring that, perhaps a fun set up for children that have been adopted out in the last few days. All of them have been, did you hear?

I did. I think finding anyone who would know about the dead will be next to impossible. They are finding records with each body, but very little information. I don't know that I mentioned it to you or not. To me, it looks like she went to a great deal of trouble, making sure she didn't get caught with the files on the children after they were dead. Jude asked if she could see what sort of paperwork it was. *Nothing much, it looks like. A name if she had it. The ones she didn't, it looks as if she put a number on them. Like the number the hospital would have assigned the infant when it was born.*

There wasn't any other way to look at this but to call it like it was. Murder. Jude had no idea how the children had been killed — she wasn't even sure she wanted to know. But they were bringing them out to be identified if they could. Otherwise, Jude knew Hanna would just be blamed for the death of Jane or John Doe, with a number after their names.

Heading to Castle Dante, the name they'd given their home, she thought about all the things she had going right now. None of it was earthshattering. It was just things she'd been putting off for too long, and now she had to hit them dead on. Damn it, she wished she had more time in the day.

Knowing more time wasn't in her future, Jude decided to enlist the help of some of the villagers of New Town. Most of them, if not all, knew more about what was needed to improve the place where they all lived. All she knew for sure was the town needed a new bank. The one there now was part of a bank system that was closing some of its branches, including the one they had in town.

Jude had spoken to the bank president, the one in charge of such matters, and he told her they were closing the branch because it was much too far for people to travel to work when the bank needed extra help. Jude had asked him when was the last time anyone had to be called in to work.

"Never. But that doesn't mean it won't happen." Jude asked him how long this particular branch had been in operation. "One hundred and sixty-seven years. We're immensely proud of that here at home office. Not a single robbery, either."

"In all that time, you've never had to have extra help, and now you're closing the place up because it still might happen? That's the stupidest thing I've ever heard. You have to see how much this bank is needed. You're the only one for a hundred miles." He told her that was precisely it. "What is? That you're the only business in a hundred miles?"

"Yes. Now you can see that it'll be much too much of a hardship for anyone to go out and fill in should they need it. My decision is made. The people there can continue to make their payments on outstanding loans via postal service. And we'll take deposits in the same way. It's not like we're abandoning them completely, Ms. Castle. They'll still be able to reach us by Internet and the phone. It's been a profitable venture in having our bank there all this time."

So the very next day, after speaking to the man, she gathered everyone up who had any business with the closing bank. Then she lent them the money to pay off their existing loans. After that, it was easy to have them close all their savings accounts as well as any other reason they might need the bank. She'd gotten a frantic call from the same bank president just this morning.

"The bank there, it has no business. Everyone in town is telling them they're going to a different bank. What have you done?" She told him what she had done, not leaving anything out. "Do you know you've cost my company a great deal of money, Ms. Castle? By paying off their loans early, those people have made it so we won't be getting the interest of the entire loan. That's a great deal of money for the banks."

"And? What's your point? You were going to hang them out to dry if they needed to get some money out of the bank for an emergency. I had to make sure my people were covered. Apparently, the bottom line is more important to you than the convenience of having good loyal customers." He told her they'd be able to get money, just not right away. "I guess you should have thought of that when you decided, quite arbitrarily, that this bank wasn't worth your time."

"But don't you see? That money coming from them was helping the bottom line for all the other branches. Not having that income, interest in the form of loans, and the savings account money, it hurts all the banks. Even the main one that I'm employed at." Jude hadn't said anything to him. "Don't you care what you've done to all of us here?"

"I care no more about how this affects you than you did about telling my people they have to wait ten business days to get money out of their account. Then to make a special effort to mail their checks to some bank thousands of miles away in time to get their loan paid off so as not to incur late charges." She laughed. "You should have thought this through, at least to the point of having someone here that is much smarter about money and people than you are. As the holder of the property of the bank you closed down, I will expect you to have the building cleared off the land within no less than thirty days of the date you close your doors."

"What do you mean, the building cleared off? Surely you meant to say cleaned out. There isn't any way I'm responsible for having a building taken down. You jest." She told him it was in the contract his company had signed all those one hundred and sixty-four years ago. "I will have to look into that. I cannot believe anyone would sign something so ludicrous as that."

"Nor would I think that a lunatic would close up a profitable bank when there was no reason for it. But that's the way it goes at times."

He called her back twenty minutes later.

"It seems as if I might have spoken too soon about the bank in that area, Mrs. Castle. We'll maintain the bank there just as we have been, and everything will go back to the way it was before." She told him no. "I'm sorry? No, what? You wish to make other arrangements with our bank? I am to assure you that we'll gladly accommodate you in any way we can. My boss has said it would not only be costly to close the branch down at this time but to have the building taken down would cost all of us a great deal of money."

"No, as in we no longer require your services as a bank

at all. You will abide by the time frame I have given you. The building will be removed, and the ground under it and surrounding it, including the parking lot, will be returned to its former condition." He sputtered around for a good minute. Jude smiled even now at how she had ended the call. "You have a lovely day, sir. And we look forward to having you erased from our town within the thirty days allotted to you."

Hanging up on him was the most satisfying thing she'd done in a while. Mostly because he was still talking about how he'd made an error in closing the bank, and that she must, as he was the only bank around, take back her time limit of having the building taken down.

Of course, she didn't answer the next calls from the same number, nor the dozen or so more she'd gotten from the same area code. She had said her piece, and he'd abide by the contract, or she'd take him to court. As soon as she saw Duncan on her way to her house, she grabbed him by both cheeks and kissed him on the mouth.

"Not that I mind that sort of greeting, but can you tell me what I did to deserve it? That way, I can do it over and over again for you." She told him about the bank. "Good. I hated that corner anyway. The building they put there was so out of place with the other buildings at the time."

"It should be gone in what I calculated as forty-one days. If it's not, I'll have Piper take it down and charge them a large fee for it. I'm not one to mess with when it comes to money." He laughed with her. "How about, since the kids aren't home, I take you home and ravish you? Sound good to you?"

"I love the way you think, my dear." He took her hand into his as they walked toward their home. "I was thinking about something a little while ago. What do you want to do about the play yard in the town square? It's been falling down for years. I never thought of getting it fixed up until I walked by it just a little bit ago."

"It's on my list. Mary is going to help me get a planning board set up to have projects like that one taken care of. Also, she's finding people to come and work at the nursery school. I hadn't any idea there was one here." Duncan said it was newly started when he'd been in town lately. "Good to know. I have a few projects I'm working on with the Over Seventy Club. Again, I had no idea there was such a thing."

"I think that's new as well." He laughed. "Do you think you and I, as well as the other birds, should join it? There isn't one of us less than a couple of thousand years old."

"You're older than even we are. Then Mary—I think she is the oldest. Did you know she has a list of people that are dependable? She's going to share it with me when we have our meeting tomorrow." Duncan said he did know about that. "I guess you would, having lived with her for so long. And you have to talk to Abe. He's having trouble adjusting to having so many people around him. Mostly it's a classroom thing, but he said he'd talk to you about something he wants. As much as I'd like to keep him home and teach him, I think he needs contact with others too much for me to give in to him."

"I'll work with him." They were home then, and he

turned to her. "I love you very much, Judith Castle. I want to say that to you all the time, and even that isn't nearly as much as I want you to know it. You are my life and my heart and soul. Thank you for being the perfect person for me."

"I love you, as well." She eyed him. "I have a feeling you're about to tell me what you've done. Is it bad? I don't want to know. Just tell me how many people I have to murder to get you out of trouble."

He opened the door. There were shouts of happy birthday from the crowd of people in the house. Closing the door on them, she glared at him.

"I swear to you, I had no idea it was going to be this big. When Mary pointed out what the date was, she figured that having you and the other birds a party would make it seem less like you guys lost my mom, and more like a rebirth of your lives. I swear to you, however. I didn't have anything to do with the planning."

Walking through the door, she could see the other birds. Going inside, she spoke to Duncan through their link.

You're losing out. You know that, don't you? He asked her what she meant. *No afternoon sex for you. I'm talking never having any in the afternoon.*

She felt his disappointment all the way across the room. Then his laughter. Standing with the other birds, she smiled, when what she really wanted to do was to knock some heads around for having this party.

Chapter 8

As soon as the party started to wind down, Duncan started cleaning up. It was busywork, really. He was debating on whether he should have told Judith as soon as the call came in, or if he, as he was doing, should have waited on the right moment to tell her. Either way, she wasn't going to be happy with the news.

"Okay, spill it." He turned and looked at his grandda when he spoke. "You've been as antsy as a cat that happened on a field of catnip. Tell me, or I'm going to send you to the woodshed. Do people do that anymore?"

"I don't think they do. Too many cameras around where people will record it then send nasty messages about you abusing the kids. Even if it was just as innocent as you taking me out there to show me something." Grandda said it was a strange world they lived in now. "You don't know the half of it, I'm afraid. I heard from the hospital. Hanna has escaped. They think her brother snuck her and himself out before she was out of recovery."

"She's that orphan woman, isn't she?" Duncan nodded. "That is a bad one, son. Really bad. You might should have told Jude when the call came in. I'd be careful of that sort of thing. Nothing can put a woman out faster than you thinking you might be protecting them when in truth, you're afraid of them. I'm afraid of your grandma. She's the sweetest thing ever created. But boy oh boy, when you piss her off, she's like a nasty snake. Getting you where it hurts you the most." Grandda shuddered and shook his head.

"I'll tell her now." Grandda told him he couldn't, she was visiting the other birds. "They were all just here together. Why does she need to visit them now? Never mind. I don't care. I'll tell her as soon as I can. Meanwhile, I want you and Grandma to be careful when you go out. You are immortal, but that doesn't mean she won't hurt you in some way."

"We'll do that. You keep my great-grandkids safe too. They don't know nothing about keeping themselves safe." Duncan thought perhaps both his kids were better at keeping themselves safe than he was. It was their only mode of survival. "Also, while I'm talking to you. I was wondering if you were serious about your grandma and me living here. I sure do like being able to just walk into another room to have a talk with you and the others."

"Grandda, I want you and Grandma here with all of my heart. Even Judith loves having you here. I know, too, that you and Abe have gotten a good relationship going.

You can stay here for as long as you want. I promise you."
Grandda hugged him tightly. It was something he was
getting used to, being hugged like he was being squeezed
in half. "You can change anything you want around here
too. We both are just so happy to have you here."

"We'll talk about changes. I was going to ask you, too,
if you'd mind if we explored some of the old caves around
here. I don't think you'd mind, but you might have a safety
reason for telling us no. We'd take the kids too if you think
they'd like that." He said the only cave he was sure they
shouldn't go in was the dark one at the top of the hill. "All
right. Can I ask you why not?"

"It's a breeding cave for some of the smaller creatures
for the area. Mostly a pip will use it for night time faeries.
But for the most part, it's used by some bats as well as a few
snakes. It's not safe to walk around other animals when
they're breeding." Grandda nodded and said it was good
to know. "You could take them to the stash too if you'd
like. I'm sure you might even find a few things of Mom's
there you'd like to keep. By the way, have you been able to
go through the stuff Mom left you in the fireplace?"

"We did. Lots of small paintings of you and her were
there. We'll treasure those—also a lot of gold. I don't know
what we'd do with it right now, but it'll be nice to know
we can fall back on it. The kids, they have anything from
the cave?" Duncan told him they didn't, just the few things
that had been given to them by the birds. "I'll see what we
can look for then. I know Miley has that set of armor. That
was nice to let her have it."

"It was. She's got a lot of things in her room that Mercy has given her too. If you wanted to take her too, she's been there. She might be able to help Abe and Tracy find something they want." Grandda thought that was a grand idea. "Great. Just let someone know when you're going, so we know when to start to worry."

"You'll worry, anyway. But in the morning I want to walk up there. I'm needing to get out more, and we'll have us a lunch there too. Spend the day going through the caves." Duncan reminded him how much colder it would be in the mountains. "Yes. I thought of that too. I'm glad you reminded me. Not a picnic, but perhaps some cookies and hot cocoa. I've not had any of that for years. Yes, I'll get on that."

Grandda was still talking to himself as he moved toward the kitchen. Duncan shook his head, thinking how much he loved having the two of them here. And Abe seemed to be coming out of his shell too. Duncan reached for Judith. He wanted her to know that Hanna was out and about so she'd not be startled if she saw her. She knew, thankfully, and didn't seem to be upset.

It was on the news. The six of us were talking about it. I don't think they're going to find her. He didn't ask. Duncan was sure he already knew the answer to why she'd not be found. *I'm tired of dicking with her. If Abe finds out she's around, he's going to hide away for the rest of his life. I want him to feel safe, no matter what.*

I agree with you. Duncan told her what Grandda and the others were doing tomorrow.

That'll be great for all of them. To get out of the house for a little while. Maybe we can work around that. I'm not sure how you feel about us —

You do what you do best, Judith. I don't want her around any more than you do. And the simple fact that she was able to escape makes me think she'll do it again until she hurts one of us. Judith told him she believed that as well. *Good. I'll not make any plans for tomorrow then. You want me to join you six?*

I think it would work better if you were to go with the others to the cave. We can handle one little human. Especially since she's got to be hurting about now. He said he could do that. *While you're there, see if you can find a painting that was in the main part of the castle. Mary said it's a painting of the sea beyond the castle walls that shows several ships out to sea. I'm not sure what else I can tell you about it, as I've never seen it.*

I think I know the one she's talking about. The ships are ours. Mom sent them out for foodstuffs, and when they returned, there was a great deal of celebration. Judith said she and the others were going to try and find the king's ship that went down. *Really? You think it's still there?*

I don't know why not. Mercy knows where it is. She's the one that put it down anyway. She said that with the king traveling, there might well be enough treasure on it to open a showing of it all. I'm thinking she just wants to make sure the fucker is dead. I'd think he was, but you know Mercy. He did and laughed with Judith. *Also, there was some jewelry on the ship. He was coming here to marry your mother, so he would have brought riches to the area to try and sway her. Not that it would have worked. But I'm betting we can find it.*

That sounds like it would be a lot of fun. Especially if we can find some of the nicer things to put in a museum, as you said. Duncan didn't think there was any other reason they'd be looking for a centuries old ship that had gone down when large stones were dropped atop it. *Is that why you left here to go there? I had no idea you were even gone.*

I came here to talk to Mercy. She's getting incredibly nervous about having a baby. None of us have ever had children before. She was freaking out a little, thinking that Joel would be upset if it was born like a bird. I think he's just thrilled to death to be getting laid on a regular basis, but that could be just me thinking outside the box. He laughed again, sitting down at his desk to work while she was gone. *I do have a question for you. When did you think we should have our own children? I'm a little nervous myself about it. I was thinking we could wait until Mercy has hers so we can all figure it out.*

I've never given it any thought, to be honest with you. It's your body, and whenever you feel the time is right, we'll work on one. In the meantime, we'll keep practicing. He smiled when she laughed at him. *I have never seen Mercy nervous. I thought she was above such feelings. I wish she was here. I'd really give her a hard time about it.*

I wouldn't. She could hurt you, king, or not. She really is a little on the intense side about this. When she laughed again, he didn't ask what was going on. She was with the others. And they forever had a great time together. *I'll see you tonight. I have a few things I want to pick up from the store on the way home. Also, before I forget again, I signed Tracy up for driver's training. She has to have it before she can get her license.*

Duncan marked his calendar with the date and times she had to be there. Judith told him Tracy didn't know about it yet, and for him to go ahead and tell her. He would too. That was another thing he added to his calendar. She'd need a safe car to be able to drive.

For the next two hours, instead of working, he was looking at cars for his daughter. Duncan thought he was enjoying that a little more than working. He had three that he really liked, and they were rated among the highest in safety. Since they all had to be ordered, Duncan ordered the three of them in different colors. He knew his grandparents needed one each, and Tracy could have first pick. When he was finished with that, he started on his paperwork.

Duncan was working on a proposal that had been given to him to open up a little floral shop near the chocolate shop in New Town when the lamp next to him shattered. It took the stuffing coming out of the back of his chair before he realized he was being shot at. Getting down on the floor, he wondered what the fuck was going on when Tracy came into the room with him.

"Get down." He was too late to save her from being shot, but she assured him it wasn't that bad. "Where is your brother? I don't want him down here to get hurt either."

"He's gone to the movie rental place with Grandda." Good. At least he was out of the house. "I have my cell. Want me to call the police, Dad?"

It startled him every time one of them called him that. But telling her no, he'd tell her mom first, had her crawling like a crab across the room towards him. The wound on her arm was bleeding pretty badly, but the bullet had gone through her arm. It was, thankfully, healing already.

Duncan tried to be as calm as he could when he reached out for Judith. She could feel his fear and anger, he was sure. When she told him they were on their way to him, all he could think about was six exceptionally large angry birds of prey coming down on whoever was out there and smashing them to smithereens. He told Tracy what he was thinking about when she asked him what was so funny.

"You don't think they'll be their big birds, do you? Holy crap, Dad. They'll bring the entire town out here to see what the heck is going on." Duncan told Tracy they'd take care of it. "Yes, I guess so. Mom, she's going to be really ticked off if one of the others saves our butts before she can. I only hope they're all safe."

The loud squawking noise was the first thing they heard. He didn't know which bird it was, but it didn't sound like anything he'd want to hear again. Then there were dark shadows that flew over the windows of the room he and Tracy were in. They both stayed on the floor, not moving around in the event the shooter hadn't been found yet. While they laid there, he told her about her driving school, as well as the cars he'd ordered for her and her grandparents.

He could feel her excitement. Duncan wasn't sure if it was the fact she was going to start driving soon or that she was going to have a new car. After he and Judith talked about her driving, they'd decided a new car for her was the best way to go, especially since she might be driving her brother around too.

When the front door opened, neither of them said anything. It wasn't until he saw a shadow that he realized it was none of the birds. Pulling Tracy to him, both of them laid there as still as they could as Hanna started toward the back of the house with a gun in her hands.

~*~

Hanna was light-headed, and she was ill. The stitches they'd put into her leg had long since come loose. She knew too that she was bleeding badly. The furnace tape that Harland had put on her was too tight, and Hanna thought she might not make it if she had to go up another flight of stairs.

She'd been able to get free of the hospital by going down a lot of stairwells. Twice she'd had to have a seat and wait a minute or two, but Harland had been right there with her with each step. Having to kill him had broken her heart, but she didn't have time to mess with him right now.

He had wanted a grilled cheese sandwich because it was Thursday, and that was the day she made them for him. It had been her fault her brothers had to have certain things made for them through the week. Having a schedule like that was the only way at times she knew what day it was. Things had been running together for some time now.

What she'd not realized, and more than likely should have, was that they would have the worst kind of fit if they didn't get what she normally would have made for them. What the hell was she supposed to do, shit him out a grilled cheese sandwich with chips? Morons. Both of them were.

Hanna had no idea where George might have been right at this time. He was in the hospital when she was taken in, but there hadn't been time to ask where she might find him. Not that it mattered. Hanna would have had to kill him too if he started in on not having anything to clean up with. She hoped wherever he had ended up, they had stock in hand cleaners. He was going to make them go broke with having to buy it all the time.

"Moron."

The stairs loomed over her. Hanna made her way to what she thought would be the kitchen instead of tackling them for the moment. There wasn't a fucking person in this place. She was sure she'd shot one of them through the window, but there didn't seem to be anyone around dead. That was all she was living for right now, to kill off that damned woman and her husband. As an added bonus, if she found the kids, she'd pop them a good one too.

Getting weaker by the moment, she sat down at the dining room table. It was a beautiful piece. The dozen chairs that lined the sides was something she would have picked out for her own home had she had one. Laying her head down on the table, she cried a little. Hanna knew she wasn't going to make it. She'd have to die without killing any of the people who had made her have to go to jail.

"I suppose I should be thrilled that you've come here to kill me. It will save me time in having to hunt your ass down. What the fuck did you think was going to happen when you got here? That we'd welcome you with open arms?" The woman sat down across from her. The rifle

Hanna had gotten from another house was just gone. "You're not getting this back, no matter how sweetly you ask me. Which, I'm quite sure you weren't going to do."

"What the hell makes you so special?" The woman, she thought her name was Jude or something like that, asked her what she meant. "This place. This is a fucking castle. Not to mention the Fort Knox amount of money you must have spent in decorating it. Why you? Why not me?"

"Okay, let me clear some things up for you. The furniture? It was made long before you were ever even thought of. I'd say about the turn of the century. Maybe before, I don't remember. The castle, it's been here longer than I have. And I'm very ancient." Hanna asked her if she thought thirty something was old. "No. But I'm much older than that. Like centuries older. Millennium older than you."

"There isn't any way you've been around that long." Jude told her it didn't matter anyway. "It does, damn it. You know I'm going to fucking die here. Why would you lie to me?"

"Yes, sorry. I'm not lying. Just like I'm not going to lie to you and tell you that a queen with a great deal of magic turned myself and five other birds of prey into larger than life birds she used to fight for and win the safety of her castle inhabitants." Hanna didn't believe her. "Which part? The birds or the age part."

"Both." Nodding once, Hanna screamed when Jude simply disappeared, and a large eagle was standing on the table between her and the chair. "I don't believe you."

The bird came to her and pecked her on the hand hard

enough to break the skin and make it bleed. As soon as the eagle went back to the chair and shifted, Jude took her hand into hers and licked the wound closed. Hanna just stared at her.

"As you can see, I can and will be a bird when I need to. As for your hand, I healed it because you're right, you're going to die here. I didn't want you to go all dark on me and not get the answers you seem to need." Five women came into the room with them. "These are the sisters of my heart. They're birds too."

Poof. That was what it looked like when the other five shifted into birds as well. Hanna couldn't take her eyes off the phoenix. She'd always thought it was a mythical bird of prey, nothing she could have counted on ever seeing in her lifetime. When they changed back, they took a seat too so that Hanna felt boxed in by them.

"The police aren't on their way to get you. They'd never make it in time anyway. I figured you'd have some questions, and we'd answer them for you." Hanna asked her why they were being nice to her. "Oh, don't get me wrong. We're not being at all nice to you. It is well within our power to make it so you don't die in my home. But we're not going to do that. We all want you out of our lives and in the dirt. This way, I won't have to explain why you were found on the property here come spring. Also, if I had wanted you dead now, you would have been before you came into the house. I'm still pissed off at you for shooting up the front of my home. And my daughter."

"You really did claim those brats?" Jude told her they

were calling her mom too. "You're appalling. Why would you want those pieces of shit in your family?"

"Watch it, old woman. I'm not as happy with you being in this house, either." She stared at the other woman. "I'm the falcon. Mercy. Which I've been told I don't have enough of. You fucking talk about my niece like that again, and even the spring thaw won't show your body."

Hanna knew she was getting too weak to argue with any of them. Laying her head back on the table, she knew she'd never get it back up again. Time and her blood were running out much too quickly.

Duncan came into the room with them. However, he didn't sit. He did ask them if they wanted anything to eat or drink. Food and drinks appeared on the table before he kissed Jude on the mouth and left. Hanna didn't bother trying to touch any of it. The thought of moving her hand to reach for something was too taxing.

"You don't have long now, Hanna. I'm not sure what else we can tell you that you'd take to the grave with you, but you're running out of time." Hanna closed her eyes. "If that's all, I'm calling the cops to come and get you."

"Why don't you bury me out back?" She thought one of them said it would spoil the earth to have her in it. "What a terrible thing to say to a dying woman. My brother, Harland, is dead. He was annoying me, so I shot him. He's in the barn out by the road. I don't remember which barn or what road. But if you sniff him out, you'll find him. George is around, I guess."

"He's in a nursing home that deals with his type of

illness." Hanna wanted to ask her what the hell she thought was wrong with him other than being stupid. But she must have understood. "He's mentally challenged. Obsessive compulsion disorder too. Did you know he's terrified of you? Or did you encourage him to be afraid of you?"

Unable to answer, she did smile. Or she thought she did. There wasn't anything left in her to open her eyes. While she could hear what was going on, there wasn't any way for her to work up the strength to answer. Hanna supposed she should have stayed in the hospital at least a couple more days. She'd have been able to do something if she had.

When she could no longer feel her legs or anything below her neck, Hanna figured she was only going to have a few seconds left to make any kind of statement. The strength it took for her to open her eye was almost too much. She looked at Jude.

"I don't...regret." Jude told her she didn't think she would. "I did...family. For us. I don't regret."

"No. Not that it matters now, but you'll pay for your deeds. I think you have a place all reserved for you in hell." Hanna thought about her being a good Christian. "I don't believe you were, Hanna. You're nothing but a nasty woman that told herself what she was doing was all in the name of family. No. You enjoyed it entirely too much for anyone to believe you now."

Hanna didn't know why she believed Jude and what she was saying, but if it were true, she thought she might well have felt differently about it while she was doing it.

Surely she had some points in her favor about her chosen way of doing things.

She had a thought. If this were a movie and someone was dying like she was, Hanna would have fast forwarded it to the end. It was boring to watch. However, she did like that she wasn't alone right now. For some reason, it gave her a little comfort knowing she wasn't lying here dying all by herself.

"Hanna, just let go. You've done enough. Just let go."

But she didn't want to. Didn't want to die all of a sudden. But the little bit of anxiety she had thinking of not wanting to do just as Jude had told her took her over the edge.

Chapter 9

Jude had so much to do today, she didn't want to get out of bed. It had been a long day yesterday, and she was ready to just throw in the towel and be lazy for about a month. Rolling to her side, she saw Duncan reading something on his phone. Taking it away from him and tossing it to the floor, she got up over his lap. His very naked lap. Jude could feel his cock stretching beneath her.

"This is a nice way to start out the day." She grinned at him. "I don't know if you're aware of this or not, or for that matter even care about it, but I've been thinking about flying you to the top of the mountains and taking you hard there."

"You can do me both here and there, can't you?" Duncan said he would die trying. "Thank you, but dying isn't going to be all right with me. But I think I needed this more than I needed anything today."

"You keep riding me like this, and I'm going to be

finished well before you will." Before she could make a comment about his lack of trying to bring her with him, he rolled her to her back and slid deep inside of her at the same time. "This is more like it. I love watching your face when you enjoy yourself."

"I enjoy myself whenever I'm near you." It was the truth. She only had to see him, and she felt better about everything. "Make me come, Duncan. I need to feel something today."

"Gladly."

He touched her everywhere as he kissed her throat and neck, and nibbled on her ear lobes. His fingers burned paths from her neck to her breast, then her hard nipples. The heat he was generating along her skin was making her shiver in anticipation. Never had a man made her feel this good about sex, nor about herself.

They didn't need words when making love. It was like their bodies spoke to each other — they told where to touch, where it needed to be pinched a little. Jude loved this man; his heart and soul were of the same cloth. A wonderful person that gave much more than he ever got. From anyone.

"You're thinking too hard." She nodded, her mouth sealed up with trying her best to hold back on the screams she wanted to release, the climaxes that seemed to be right there on the edge of some kind of pinnacle. "Let it go, Judith, my love. Let me be a witness to you coming apart just for me."

She could no more have held back if she'd been falling over the cliff. Her body didn't just come apart, but seemed to pause, just for a few seconds, so that she was positive she'd never be the same again.

Coming back into herself, Jude felt every nerve ending come alive. She felt as if she'd been set in warm water and then a live wire set in it with her. Screaming didn't just spill from her mouth and throat—she could feel the sound of it coming from her toes. Beyond them, if there had been such a place.

"Again." It seemed to be his word for her. Every time he said it, even to start to say the word, her body would bow up nearly in half, and she'd be coming again. "That's it, love. Show me all you have."

She had nothing left, she thought each time she released. There wasn't a drop of energy in her at all. But when he told her to come, she did so with such vigor, such all-out everything she had, Jude knew she was going to hurt in the morning. If she lived that long.

When Duncan started to take her harder, his body pounding hers like he was going to push her along with him, Jude held onto him. Not just with her hands dug deep into his shoulders, but by wrapping her legs around him to make sure she knew where to return when he let her off at the end of his ride.

When he did come, his body pouring into hers, Jude watched his face. It looked as if he were carved from stone, his face was so set. When his fingers dug into her meaty flesh at her ass, she knew she was going to be bruised, sorer than she'd ever been before. However, it was his look of love that made her feel as if she were everything to him.

His world, his light. Jude came, screaming again when he told her to. Then there wasn't anything.

When she woke, the room was dark. She'd slept all day? Getting up, heading to the bathroom to get cleaned up, her watch told her what her body was already saying. It was nearly midnight. She'd slept the clock around today.

I wondered if you were going to rise anytime soon. Jude told Duncan he should have woke her. *I tried, believe me. I really tried. But you were out like a stone had hit you, and there wasn't any movement at all from you.*

I've never slept the entire day away. I must have really needed it. He told her it had been three days. *I slept for three days? Not possible.*

Not only is it possible, but I think you were right. You must have needed it. I would check on you when I was home several times a day. But you weren't even dreaming that I could find. I swear, a couple of times, I'm sure Abe and Tracy thought I'd killed you. It got to the point where they were checking on you as well. She told him that was sweet. *Yes, it also kept me from having to explain to the police why you were out like you were. I think Tracy might already know. She's been winking at me since she checked on you a couple of times.*

Oh my. Duncan only said yes. *Well, I guess we don't have to worry about whether or not she knows about sex. Let me take a shower, and I'll be down. Is there anything I need to know while I'm getting three days of sleep off me?*

One thing, and it's important. The president of the Bank of America will be here in the morning. I was going to have to let one of the other birds take the meeting with him, so I'm glad you finally got up. She said she didn't want to miss it. *Good. He's been genuinely nice just so you know. Asking about the family. New Town. I think he's going to try and butter you up to take their bank back. Are you?*

No. *I mean, we've already figured out we don't need to have a bank here. Paying their fees is how they make payments for their board members. Without the bank there to turn anyone down on things, we've had a surplus of remodels going on in houses. Two new builds, as well as three new businesses going in because we approved them rather than the bank turning them down. The only reason they had for not giving these loans was, they were thinking anyone that works for themselves isn't going to be diligent at paying them back when the time comes. The other banker didn't seem to take into account how long these people and their descendants have lived, worked, and died here.* Duncan said he'd been turned down for a loan as well. *What were you needing money for? If you don't mind me asking.*

I was trying to stimulate things around here. You know, borrow money so the bank could have more to use for my fellow neighbors. I didn't need anything. I was just trying to get things going. But, as you said, I don't have a job where they can actually see me going to work every day, and I was turned down. As she was drying her hair, she had a sudden odd feeling. Like her body was being revved up. *I can feel that. I think I know what it is too. Your body will be like that forever. I feel like that every day. I don't sleep either.*

Would she enjoy that? Never having to sleep again? It would certainly help her get more things done during the day. And some of the things she didn't need to work on, but would just enjoy doing. Like painting again. It had been her way to relieve stress since she'd been turned.

Going down to the kitchen, she was glad to see it was just Duncan in the big room with her. There was a tray of sandwiches on the table, as well as several kinds of fruit in two smaller bowls. She picked up a piece of cantaloupe and ate it while he poured the two of them something to drink.

"You're going to need to eat more fresh fruits and vegetables now if this is what that power surge coming from you was. Also, you're not going to like this, but you can't just squeeze more into your day. You have to temper this being awake all the time with just as much rest as you were getting before. Otherwise, you'll burn yourself out." She told him she'd not seen him resting. "Ah, but I do. When you're asleep, I take my downtime. I learned the hard way about burning myself out. I was going so much I never knew if I was coming or going. My days blended together, and I went a little nuts. Not a little nuts, but big time. I wasn't finishing projects. I began to see things that weren't there. Several times I thought I was being stalked when it was only my mind playing tricks on me because it was exhausted from trying to keep up with me. You'll figure it out, or it will incapacitate you for a long time. But you'll only do that the one time. It's that hard on you."

She remembered then when they'd all been working on getting the village moved to New Town. Dante had been going and going until she simply collapsed one day. After that day, she was weak and out of sorts. It never occurred to her until now that Dante hadn't been resting, but working throughout the night when the rest of them did take some downtime. Jude asked Duncan if he knew if his mother had slept.

"I don't know for sure. But there were times when she'd come to see me, and I'd have to be awakened. Back then, when I was younger, I did sleep. After Mom died, I never had the need for it." Jude told him she'd be careful. She also told him the story about his mom. "I'd like for you to do that when you think of something. I didn't know her the way you and the other birds did. I knew her as my mom and not the queen she was. I'll even tell you all things she said to me about you. It was never anything but praise. Sometimes she'd tell me how one of you, mostly Mercy, would get on her about this or that. While she didn't like it, I think she respected all of you for loving her enough to make sure she was safe."

"Thank you for that. I have plenty of stories about her I could tell you. I thought of something else just now. Your mother was already dead when we destroyed the castle." Duncan looked at her, his face filled with hope. "I know she took a poison before she summoned us to destroy all while she was in it. We didn't want to, but she told us, and we knew she was right—that if this king were to make it here, she'd be dead anyway. She knew as well as we did, he wasn't going to keep her around. He only wanted the castle and the lands and people here. I believe she also knew that Mercy, in her grief, would destroy the ship he was coming here in."

"Mom didn't tell me that part in her letters to me, about

where she died first. She only explained to me why it had to be done. And how. If the castle was destroyed, then no one would think anything of looking for her people. With her dead inside, it would look as if she was set upon and had died defending it." Jude nodded. "The people being gone too would have made it look as if they'd been taken captive and were more than likely all dead too. I need to know these things. All the information about her. This was a good story, Jude, and it cleared my heart of thinking of her suffering, even a little when the walls came down. Thank you for this."

"It's my pleasure, Duncan." She ate some of the sandwich but did prefer the fruit. As a bird, she didn't really get much in the way of fresh fruit as she did as a human. "Something else I want you to know about your mom. She wasn't perfect, not even close. Dante made a great many mistakes when she was queen. She also was stubborn as hell about things. But she would admit, readily, when she was wrong and would say she was sorry right away. Nor did Dante hold a grudge. You should know too, when she was right about a plan or project, it was epic. And she'd make sure we celebrated those victories very well."

"I knew that about her. She was never one to say she told you so either." Jude told him that was right. "Thank you again, Jude. I wish there were more pictures of the two of us sometimes. I understood the reasoning behind her hiding me away. What I have trouble with is how she was able to keep her pregnancy so quiet."

"She used magic, I would imagine. She had a great

deal of it. Dante could make a person see what she wanted them to see — or not see, in this case. I'm sure she had your father believing she never conceived or had a child, even if he was in the room with her when she birthed you." Jude laughed. "Your mom could never make it work on any of us. There wasn't any reason for her not to have been able to trick us, but she couldn't do it anyway. I used to think it was because she created us. I don't know. But it is nice to know she couldn't."

"Nor me. Mary, yes, but never me. The only reason I'm sure of it is because she told me how she was making Mary rest more. For her to go to certain merchants when Mom was in need of something she didn't want others to know about. I believe it was mostly potions and such. Mom could cast too if she needed to." Jude knew that, as well. "Well, my dear. What do you have to do today?"

"Several things, actually." She handed him the list she'd started in the bathroom this morning. "Tracy has decided she wants to take some college classes online, so we need to get her registered for that soon."

After telling him her list, Duncan pulled up his phone. She knew she should be more fluent with the phone and what it could do for her. Jude just didn't care all that much to do it. Someday, she'd kept telling herself. Well, it was, in her opinion, too much to learn now. Besides, she had her own method, and it worked well for her.

Laughing at Duncan's attempts to get her up on the latest things, she left the house and him with a short kiss. There really was a lot to be said for having a paper list. She could simply scribble it out when she was finished with it. He could only delete.

~*~

Going over the paperwork that had been on his desk since Christmas, Duncan concentrated on each word this time in order to make sense of what it was saying. There was something there, some word that was out of place that he knew was going to trick him up. After reading it several more times, he put it down when a happy distraction entered the room with him.

"Tracy. Thank goodness you're here." She laughed, and he smiled at her. "I have this paperwork, contract I guess you'd call it, for the new building that we're putting in. It's going to be for things like large gatherings, as well as plays and such for all the grades." She sat down and took the paperwork. "I think I'm reading more into this than there is, but for some reason, it's eluding me as to what I'm missing."

"What do you mean?" Duncan explained it to her as best he could. "So, you think there is some sort of magic on the page that is keeping you from reading it properly?"

"I'd never thought of that. Yes, that might be it in a nutshell. It's hiding something from me. I was wondering if you could see what I can't." She looked it over, then looked up at him. "You've found it, haven't you?"

"Before I tell you the answer, there is something I need to tell you first. I went to speak to Mercy yesterday. I told her how I was worried that people might take advantage of me now. You know, people have to know that you and

Mom have money. I asked Mercy what I could do to prevent magic from being used on me to fall in love with a dead beat jerk and things like that. Understand?" Duncan told her he could have done it for her. "Yes, but like Mom, you would have wanted to know who had done such a thing to me, and would have been ready to hunt them down. This was a preventive thing, not someone taking me to the cleaners now."

He smiled at her, and she grinned. "I believe you know us all too well. Okay, so Mercy helped you with this magic. I'm assuming she told you to tell us about it." Tracy told him she had been very stern about letting them know. "Good for her. And for you for making sure you knew when someone was pulling something like that on you. What does it say, honey?"

"Mostly, it's just what you'd think in a contract, except for this little bit in the middle. Right here, it says this. 'If the project runs too long, there will be no consequences made to the builders. And if there is any leftover material, no matter the cost, it will be given to the builders at no charge to them.' I'm thinking if they're doing the ordering, you're going to be in the red for an exceedingly long time on this project." As he took the papers back, she went on to explain something else to him. "There are a couple of other benefits to the builders there. Mostly it's what I thought about them doing the material ordering, as well as they hire as many men as they need to finish the project. For that alone, even knowing it's in there, I'd not hire them. I would like to work with you on more projects so that I can run them too."

"You want to work with me?" She said for him. "No. You're my daughter. And someday I'd like for you to take over a lot of the projects. As my oldest, it would fall to you to take them anyway."

"I'm not your child. I mean, biologically, I'm not of your blood." Duncan set the papers on his desk and looked at her. "I know I'm going to have to take some hits in that I'm not your daughter. I think, and I'm sure this is true that you took me under your roof because of Abe. And I'd—"

"Stop right there. Have I treated you as if you're nothing more to me than someone I took in?" She said he'd been really nice to her. "Good. I'd hate to think that with my first child, I'd mess up that badly. Tracy, as far as I'm concerned, you're my child. Blood or not, I won't treat you any differently than I would a child born to myself and Jude. I love you—both you and Abe. You have no idea how much I look forward to things that I'll be asked to do as your father. And I am. The same as if I had raised you from birth."

She turned away, then looked at him again. There were tears on her cheeks, and his heart hurt for them. Standing up, he came around the desk and held her in his arms when she stood up. It was as if holding her brought the doors to the dam wide open. She sobbed against his chest like she'd been holding them in for a while now.

"I've been on my own for so long. Even living in the home so I could take care of Abe, I was still alone. I never dreamed, at my age, that anyone would love me. Not like a child of their own. Never as a woman falling in love with a man. Then you and Mom came along and opened so many doors for me. I will tell you, I kept waiting for one of you to slam them shut in my face. Every time I speak to you, I think this will be the time you tell me it's been a joke." Duncan told her he'd never do that. "I know in my head you wouldn't. However, my heart is waiting for the day you come to your senses and kick me to the curb."

"Never. Besides, I think even if that thought came into my head, one of the birds would take me to the highest peak in the world and kick me off to see me crushed on the rocks below. I won't tell them this, but they scare me." Laughing, Tracy looked up at him. "There. That's what I wanted to see—a smile from my firstborn. Tracy, I love you. Very much so. You're my daughter, and I'd be honored if you would work with me. But never when you have homework."

"I promise, homework and life is first."

He held her tightly and saw Jude in the doorway. "She was feeling a little insecure. I thought a hug would take care of that. You have one for her?"

"I do, as a matter of fact." Jude came and hugged the two of them tightly. "My goodness. I never thought of anything I'd love as much as being a bird. But this, right here and right now, makes all the things I had to go through to be a human all very worthwhile."

They stood there, hugging and saying how much they had grown to love hugs. Tracy was no longer crying. She also looked more like she believed them. Duncan went to sit at his desk when she pulled away. His heart, for the first time in longer than he could remember, felt tender and wounded that she'd believed he'd ever let her leave.

Jude came to look over some of the other reports they'd gotten in the mail today. Mostly it was people wanting to borrow money for their projects. Each of them would be considered and looked into. The first one on top of the list was one he thought they could use right now. But both Tracy and Jude disagreed.

It was for a new library, as well as reading space. An addition of some computers was also on the list. He asked them why they thought it was a bad idea. Jude answered him first, but he could tell that Tracy didn't agree with her ideas either.

"We have a library here." He asked Jude how long it had been since it had been updated. "That I couldn't tell you, but I do know they're getting books in weekly they set out for people to read."

"I think the reading space is a good idea. But without walls. Well, we could have walls, but only in the colder months." Duncan asked Tracy what she had in mind. "I love to read. I'm sure you guys do as well. There are enough books in this place to put any library to shame. However, I know for a fact you can buy readers, several of them, and put an infinite amount of books on them. Erase the ones you've read to make more downloadable. That's what I use. As for the having no walls, there could be a lovely park to read in. Chairs set in different places around the park. Easily moved ones a person could take with them to read in their favorite spot. A place to have quiet time. A brook that might be making just enough noise so that a person could nap should they need it. A refuge, I guess you could call it."

"I love that idea. I can see a lot of people using it." Tracy said that children would have their own park, with animals and such to play with. "Yes, I'm loving this so far. I think it's a brilliant idea."

"However, no computers in the park or in the reading area. The readers are only used for reading. No online searches while out in the park. No Wi-Fi, I think. A place that can be used simply to wind down. Step back from the electrical age." Duncan asked her what made her think of this. "The other day, I was in the little park that was made for Dante. I just realized she's my grandmother. Anyway, I was there, just smelling the different flowers and reading about the trees. A bunch of kids, about Abe's age, came into the little space and turned on their phones to play music. It was disheartening to know they were only there because their parents had kicked them out of the house for quiet time for them. The kids were talking about how their parents weren't into their music. I didn't mind the style; I did mind the volume."

"We could put in a media room too." Tracy nodded and thought it was a good idea. As the two of them tossed ideas back and forth, he set the library addition aside. Pulling up the next paper, he looked at it for five minutes before he realized neither of the women were speaking. They were looking at him with an odd look on their faces.

"What are you upset about?" He asked Jude how she'd come to that. "You're talking to yourself. Actually, you're cursing too, but it was the talk that had us looking at you. What's going on with whatever you're looking at?"

"Do you remember Mr. Bloom? He was here at Christmas. Remember how he and Abe connected well?" Jude mentioned how she'd taken Abe to his house a few times last week. "Yes, that's right. Well, he passed away the day before yesterday. Abe and Tracy are mentioned in his will."

"Me? Why me? I mean, in a will, does that mean I might owe him something? Because if it does, I'm not going. I doubt even Abe would go." Duncan told her that all it said was they were mentioned. "Can you find out?"

"I'll check, but I doubt you owe him anything. Usually, when someone is mentioned in a will, they're going to get something. Not the other way around. The person has died, so I'm thinking he doesn't believe you owe him anything." Tracy glared at him. "And that is such a teenager thing to do, love."

"Good. I'm not sure what he'd be leaving us. To be honest, I didn't talk to him as much as Abe did. And the one time I was there with my brother, he offered me his library to use while they worked on a project the two of them had started." She looked hopeful. "Do you think he might have left me some of his books? He has a—had a large collection of all sorts of books."

"We'll have to find out by going to the attorneys tomorrow. We're to be there at ten in the morning. Is there anything going on that I need to know about first?" Jude told him nothing, and Tracy said she had a test for school, but it wasn't until later in the day at three. "I'm thinking we should be done in plenty of time for you to make that class."

After they left him to his work, he was able to finish up on two more projects. Duncan was glad for the help in getting through the paperwork. Jude had taken half of his workload and had finished most of them already. He would be glad when he was caught up. Then he'd only have one or two a day to deal with instead of the four dozen or so he'd been putting off in favor of the holidays, as well as getting the castle ready for he and Jude to live in.

Chapter 10

Jude watched the line running through the building before she had them shut it off. Something was off here, and she knew it had to do with human error rather than anything with the lines. So far, she'd been able to track five packages, and each of them had gone to the correct line to be loaded onto the right truck. She turned when Remi said her name.

"Did you know when we got here today that there was over a million dollars in missing product?" Jude told her she'd found it already. "How? And you should have said something, damn it. I have other shit I can be doing if I'm only here to chase your fucking tail. I've been looking for over two hours."

"What's the matter?" Remi asked her what she meant. "You've been snapping and biting since you got here. I can only imagine what you said to any of the employees. This isn't like you. What's up?"

Remi opened her mouth but closed it immediately before letting out a long breath. Remi, short for Remington, sat down on the floor. When she shifted to her other self, a vulture, Jude cocked a brow at her. Something really was off if she'd rather be a bird than to speak her mind. As soon as she changed back, Jude joined her on the floor.

"Three nights ago, I was flying over New Town. I was seeing how far my new home was going to be from the castle. It's not far, but I saw you out in the yard talking to Tracy. Who I love, by the way." Jude said that Tracy loved her as well. "I'm super jealous."

"Because I have a back yard I can speak to someone in? I'm sure you can have a back yard as well." Remi growled. "Doesn't work on me. Not that it ever did, but tell me or go away. I don't have time for your bullshit, nor you having a childish temper tantrum."

"I want a child of my own. I don't want a mate. I don't have time to clean up after them. But I want a kid I can take out to lunch when I want to go. Someone to go shopping with. Stuff like you do with Tracy." Jude asked her what she was talking about. "A kid I can have fun with."

"Okay, first of all, you do know you could call up Tracy, and she'd go to the ends of the earth with you." Remi said it wasn't the same thing. "I guess not. But have you seen the work that Mercy is doing for her new baby? A lot more than I think you want to invest in a kid to have lunch with. Besides, I think it'll be an exceptionally long time before the kid can eat food, much less read a menu to order from."

"Stop being an ass and help me." Jude told her she was.

"I don't want a baby, dumb ass. I want a kid. Like Tracy."

"You want someone to pull out when you're bored and need someone to go with you." Remi started shaking her head. "Yes, that's all you're talking about. I'm sure if you got a kid like Tracy, you'd find out that it's a lot of work to have them want to go anyplace with you. Tracy is driving soon, and I'm betting I don't get to have fun with her much more. She'll be hanging with her own friends then."

"That kid worships you." Jude told Remi she did her too. "But she's not mine. I want what you have."

"I'd like to tell you that's sweet, but it's not what you want. I mean, think about what you're saying to me. You want a kid. You want to go shopping with it. You want to have fun. What about what this kid is going to want?" Remi frowned like she was confused. "Tracy trusts me not to leave her at the side of the road when we're finished with lunch. You haven't mentioned the child staying with you. Twenty-four seven. That's what you get when you have a kid. Also, you neglected to mention things like shopping for her. Or buying food so that it's in the house when you're not with her. What do you think this kid is going to do when you're wrapped up in your work and can't be going out with her? Usually, kids start out as infants and grow into the children that Tracy and Abe are. Are you really that bored you want a child to rear? Or do you want to handpick someone to be your companion?"

"I don't know now." Jude stood up and helped Remi up. "I'm not going to be any good at raising a family, Jude. I don't want babies around. I don't want to even think about having one either. I love my life the way it is. I get to make food for the restaurant, then watch to see if people like it or not. From what you're saying, this kid will also judge me."

"Yes, they do. I am incredibly lucky in that I have Tracy now. In a couple more years, she's going to be off to college. Maybe find a man to love her, as well as have children of her own. Not for a long time yet, but it's in her future." Remi nodded. "Also, what if you find your mate and you find out he hates kids? And especially the one you picked up to have lunch with you. What will you do then?"

"He will not come between me and my child." Jude laughed when Remi shouted about that. "Okay, you've made your point. I need to think about what I really want in life, and understand there are consequences with my choices."

"I was serious when I told you to take Tracy when you want someone to hang around with. Abe, too if you want. He's the best person to have a long discussion with. It doesn't even have to be about anything in particular. Abe is smart, and he has all sorts of opinions on a great many things." Remi asked if she was serious. "About Abe? Yes. He goes out with Duncan's grandda a couple of times a week. Even his grandma comes over and gets him when she's onto her next big project."

"I think I might take you up on that. I mean, really. He's a great kid, and he is smart." Jude nodded. "All right. I'm ready to figure this out now. What's going on with the lines? I'm sure you've not only figured it out, but you also know how to fix it."

"Look above you." Jude watched the line she was set to watch as Remi watched the lines coming between the two rooms. As soon as she saw what Jude had found after coming here for a couple of days, Remi looked at her. "I don't know where he lives when he's not stealing boxes from the line, but I have to put a stop to it. I wonder if other faeries are living in this place that are making it their home."

"I'd say there are. He isn't incredibly sneaky about his theft, is he? I mean, he didn't bother hiding himself when he noticed I was looking at him." Jude told her how he'd been in the break room when she'd been there. "Did he speak to you?"

"No. I think he's realized I'm the queen and he's afraid of me. I'm also thinking if he's having to steal whatever he takes, he needs a job as well." Remi asked her what she had in mind. "It's why I brought you along with me. You can talk to him without him being terrified. I was hoping he'll speak to you easier than he would me."

Remi waited for the faerie to come out on the line again and yelled at him to meet her in the dining area. When she winked at her and left, Jude wondered how this would end. Remi wasn't a straight to the point speaker. It took her longer to tell a joke than anyone wanted to wait for the punch line.

After about twenty more minutes of watching the line, Jude made her way to the office and sat at her desk to await Remi. She'd have to leave here soon, she realized. Duncan had been called out of town right after he'd left the house.

He'd not have been able to make the meeting this morning, even if he'd been able to leave on time. Sometimes it sucked to be in charge of large operations. Smiling, she wondered what he'd say when he returned, and she told him about the faerie.

She didn't know his name. However, what she did know about him was a lot. He'd been stealing things from right off the lines for some time now—about ten years, she thought. It wasn't just food either. He'd been taking supplies to make things as well. It was why she thought there was more than just the one of them in the building.

Yesterday's inventory showed that there were six bags of cotton filling missing, as well as ribbons of silk and scissors. Also, several bags of weaving material were gone. It didn't seem like a great deal daily, but adding it up over the last ten years, it had amounted to a great deal. As soon as Remi entered her office, Jude could tell that whatever was going on, it was going to continue.

"This is Patch. Patch, you're with the queen now, so behave yourself." Patch nodded, then bowed to her. "Patch has a wife and three children. Also, by his count, there are about four hundred families of faeries living in the upper levels of this place. He's been helping them out by getting them supplies to set up a home."

"Why are you the only one taking the things? I'd think with four hundred families, you'd be working all the time doing it alone." He looked at Remi before bowing to her again. "Patch, I'd like to not have to tell the king about this if I can get it taken care of today."

"They be older, my lady." She asked him what he meant. "The others, the others in the pip. They're no longer able to work. The places they worked at, me too, have been closed down. The faeries, they're not useful to many anymore."

"Where did they work before coming here? Where did they work that has closed down?" Patch told her about the greenhouse that had been closed up for some years now. They all had worked there and didn't know anything else to do. "They have only ever been greenhouse workers — is that what you're telling me?"

"Yes, my lady. They don't know how to do nothing else. Most of them, me included, where born in the building that served the greenhouse. When it was closed down, it nearly killed all of us until we found this place. It wasn't nothing like it is now, so I've had to help them all move several times when the work started up here." He looked at her like he was thinking it was her fault. "I don't know what to tell you about the stuff I've been taking. But we were here first."

"So you were. Yes, I can see that. All the families here, are they willing to work for a living?" His face was so bright with excitement; she nearly smiled with him. Then his face seemed to sadden. "I'll not lie to you if you do the same for me, Patch. I have work for you and your people — more too if they need it."

"What kind of work are you saying to?" She told him of the great greenhouse she had at the castle. "We'd be working for you, my lady? At the castle?"

"Yes. The greenhouse will be magical, of course. I will

need all of you there to pick what is ready and help with the management of the seeds we have. Some of them are as old as we are, Patch. They'll need special care from incredibly special people." He said he could do that. "I know you can. I'm counting on it. Also, there will be food and things that can be used for homes for all of you. I'll make sure of it. The things they have here—do you think it will take a great deal to load them up and take to their new jobs?"

"No, my lady. We can take care of that. When do you want us to start?" She told him as soon as they were all settled in the greenhouse. "My lady, this is most wondrous. I don't know what to say."

"Tell me you'll do a good job. Because the things that are grown in the greenhouse will help a great many people. Fruits and vegetables will be readily given to humans that would die without the proper foods. Older humans that have no way to grow things as you would do, because they're only humans and don't have the energy they once had. Or, and this is true in most of the cases, they no longer have the soil to work the seeds into."

"That's just terrible. Terrible so much." She didn't bother correcting his English. Patch might be one to take offense to it. "I'll gladly tell the others we're moving. If you could mayhap get us a conveyance, we can move out of here today."

"I can have a truck for you today. However, I need to go to another appointment. You can work it out with the others, and I'll be expecting you to come by the castle once everyone agrees to help us out." He said he'd do it. "All right then. Thank you for your help, Patch. You'll make a wonderful foreman for us."

Making her way to the garage to get into her car, she told Remi how to handle the move. Remi was laughing so hard at the things Patch was telling her that she was repeating it all to her. The little man was making some small demands about the move that had them both nearly in stitches, laughing so hard. He wanted each person to have a shoebox to have their things put into so they'd not be hurt. Also, he wanted cotton to wrap any delicates in. Remi was giving him everything he needed to make the move go easier on them all.

Jude walked into the attorney's office right on time. Tracy was already there with Abe, having gotten a ride from Grandpa. He said he'd go on home now, and the attorney asked if he'd like to stay and listen. Grandpa was incredibly happy to do so since he had a lunch date with his favorite children.

Whatever was going to happen here today, the attorney, Mr. Shelby, was excited about it. As they were taken to the room for the reading, Duncan joined them. She'd never been so happy to see him as she was in that moment. His meeting, he told them, had been canceled. Thankfully.

~*~

Abe didn't know what to expect with this. He watched Tracy for her reaction, and when she was calm, so was he. So far she'd been very calm, and he was glad for that. Mr. Bloom had been a good friend to him, someone he could talk to without worrying he was going to judge him afterward.

"You're a smart boy, aren't you?" He didn't answer him, knowing that if people found out how smart he really was, they'd make fun of him. "You should tell them parents of yours. They'll get you into some classes that won't leave you snoozing on the sidelines."

"I love living with them. I don't want to be turned out again." Mr. Bloom asked him if he really thought they'd do that. "No. But I don't want to have to worry that they will. It's what my parents did. They didn't like that I was smarter than them. So when they went to prison, and I went to the home, I met Tracy. We needed each other."

"I don't know your new folks that well, but they don't strike me as the type that wouldn't be shouting to the mountain tops bragging on you a little."

Abe had grinned, but he wasn't sure what to do. Even now, all these weeks later, he'd still not told them.

Now here he was in an attorney's office wondering what the older man had left him. Not that he wanted anything. He wanted the friendship to continue, but it was over now. The elderly man had passed away in his sleep.

"Abraham Dante." He looked at the well-dressed man when he said his name. "Mr. Bloom thought a great deal of you and your sister. But he especially loved you. He said that had he had a chance to have any children he wanted, he would have picked you and your sister, Tracy. He was a good man, too, you know."

"I know. He and I would have talks all the time about how things worked when he was younger. I loved him so much." The man nodded. "He didn't have to leave me anything. I just liked being around him. Whatever it is, it won't mean as much to me as having him as a friend."

"I think he said you'd say that. But what he left you is his house, and the property surrounding it. Also, you're going to be the owner of all his vines. Did he tell you he was a winemaker?" Abe said he'd shown him how it worked. "Yes, Mr. Bloom told me he did that. Said you'd understand things he told you and how to make it work, so you didn't have to work all that hard."

"That's a lot of vines. Don't you think?" Mr. Shelby told him it was. "I'm just a little boy. I don't know how to do enough yet."

"That's why he's going to have your dad here help you. There are also people that will help you learn the job so you'll be as good if not better than he was at it. Mr. Bloom told me if anyone could make it work, it would be you." Abe was touched by the thought of the elderly man. "After we're finished up here, I'll go over the contracts with you and your dad so you can start on it as soon as tomorrow. The people working the winery are happy you're going to be running the place for him."

Mr. Shelby looked at Tracy. She, too, said she didn't want anything from Mr. Bloom. But Mr. Shelby told her that it was his pleasure to tell her what she'd been left by the older man.

"He left you his money. All of his shares in all his companies too. You both are very wealthy. He figured that by the end of this year, both of you will have turned what he left you into so much more." Tracy asked about his family. "There is no one to fight with you over what he's done. They're all gone, his family. There weren't any children from his union with his wife either. He was a good man who was never blessed, he called it, with anyone he could call his own until you two came along."

"I don't understand." Abe looked at Tracy and thought she was dense if she didn't get that she had all the money. "I'm incredibly happy with what he's done, but we just met him at Christmas. I don't know how we could have made an impression on him that quickly, do you?"

"Mr. Bloom made all his money when he was in his late sixties. His wife had passed on by then, and it seemed that anything he touched turned to gold. Even when he tried to make himself lose money, he would triple whatever he'd put into it. And a good thing too." He winked at Abe. "As of this morning, when the paperwork came to me, you're worth more than seventy million dollars. Ms. Tracy, you are worth a little more, but he said you'd be sharing with your brother anyway, so he made sure you had plenty to do that. He has plans for you both, as a matter of fact. Nothing that will take away the money, never that, but he wanted you both to be able to go to college and not have to worry about money. He also wanted to make sure you both lived close enough to your parents so you could go to them for not just advice, but hugs too. Mr. Bloom told me that Tracy gave the best hugs he'd ever had."

By the time they were finished with the will, Abe was terrified. Not of the money, but that someone was going to ask him what all had been said at the meeting. By the time they were having lunch, Grandpa with them, he was starting to realize that this was real and that he was going to be running some very wonderful companies. As soon as his food was brought to him, he turned to his parents and told them what he'd promised Mr. Bloom he would do.

"I need to be retested for school. I didn't do it right." Dad asked him what he meant. "I'm smart. Too smart for me to be in fifth grade. I have trouble, you see, paying attention when I know more than the teachers do. They never let me go and do homework that was in the higher grades, so I'd have to stay where I was and not do anything like I wanted."

"So, you dumbed yourself down for the classes you were in." He nodded. "All right. We can take care of that in the morning."

"Are you mad at me?" Mom asked him why he'd think that. "I don't know. The teachers at the home said I was a showoff and didn't like it when I had the correct answer. Even when they didn't have it right. They were forever mad at me."

"I'm not. Not at all. I'm thrilled to death that you are smart. Now I don't have to help you with your homework." Abe laughed and said he'd help her. "You might have to, you know. I never got to go to school when I was made. I took college classes, but I never went to grade school or above."

They talked about it all through lunch and on the way home. He had a lot to think about, and Abe was going to make sure that Mr. Bloom hadn't done anything wrong by leaving them the money. He was going to make it show for something good.

At least he hoped so.

Before You Go...

HELP AN AUTHOR

write a review

THANK YOU!

Share your voice and help guide other readers to these wonderful books. Even if it's only a line or two, your reviews help readers discover the author's books so they can continue creating stories that you'll love. Log in to your favorite retailer and leave a review. Thank you.

AWARD WINNING, BESTSELLING AUTHOR

Kathi Barton, a winner of the Pinnacle Book Achievement award as well as a best-selling author on Amazon and All Romance books, lives in Nashport, Ohio, with her husband, Paul. When not creating new worlds and romance, Kathi and her husband enjoy camping and going to auctions. She can also be seen at county fairs with her husband, who is an artist and potter.

Her muse, a cross between Jimmy Stewart and Hugh Jackman, brings her stories to life for her readers in a way that has them coming back time and again for more. Her favorite genre is paranormal romance, with a great deal of spice. You can visit Kathi on line and drop her an email if you'd like. She loves hearing from her fans. aaronskiss@gmail.com.

Follow Kathi on her blog: http://kathisbartonauthor.blogspot.com/

www.ingramcontent.com/pod-product-compliance
Lightning Source LLC
Chambersburg PA
CBHW020624180626
46810CB00007B/2915